Falling for a Devoted Cowgirl

VARGAS RANCH BOOK 6

Karen Baney

desert life
media

With regard to the works of man,
by the word of your lips
I have avoided the ways of the violent.
My steps have held fast to your paths;
my feet have not slipped.

Psalms 17:4-5 ESV

1

"ADAN FRANCO?"

ADAN heard the unfamiliar man's voice behind him. Without looking up from picking Pansy's hoof, he answered.

"We ask that all guests wait outside. The horses are almost ready."

The man cleared his throat. "I'm not a guest."

Adan eased Pansy's clean hoof to the floor of the grooming area before placing his palm lightly on her side. He strode to her rear hoof, then he propped it on his leg.

"Then you really shouldn't be in here."

"Sir, are you Adan Franco?"

Adan breathed deeply to calm his irritation. The smell of hay and horse hung heavy in the air. What should have been a peaceful afternoon had already gone off the rails before this interruption. Adan moved the pick over Pansy's rear hoof, digging out the bits of dirt and hay that had accumulated since her last grooming.

"Sir?"

Taking another deep breath, Adan lowered Pansy's clean hoof. He kept his hand on her, near the base of her neck, before he looked up. A man in a full-blown suit, tie, and everything stood at the entrance of the grooming area. Adan's heart beat in double time when his gaze flicked away from the man to the boy standing next to him. His ire grew. It wasn't good to bring kids unfamiliar with horses back there, even if the kid wore a cowboy hat and boots.

"Yes, I'm Adan Franco. Now, if you don't mind, please take the boy and yourself out of here."

"We need to talk."

"About?"

"I'd rather not say in front of an audience."

"Go," Dylan said. "I'll finish up with Pansy. You can use my office."

Adan nodded sharply, patted Pansy, and stepped back. Then he swiveled on his booted heel, frowning at Mr. Suit. "This way."

Adan led the man and boy down the alleyway to Dylan's office in the back of the stables. He nudged the door open, hinges groaning in response. Then he flipped on the lights and motioned to the guest chairs. Though it felt weird to sit in Dylan's chair, he did anyway. Just the way the seating worked out.

"Am I in some sort of legal trouble?" he asked, mind working over who would wear a suit to meet with him. Lawyer made the most sense.

"Not exactly." Mr. Suit cleared his throat. "I'm Mr. Edward Haynes. Attorney for the estate of..." He gulped a deep breath before pushing out the words. "Annabel Garrison."

The name hit Adan hard in the solar plexus, nearly knocking him into next week. He remembered Annabel. Pretty gold eyes and strawberry blond hair. She had been a barrel racer on the same rodeo circuit he used to...

Wait a second. "Estate?"

Haynes nodded and reality started to sink in, pushing Adan's stomach down around his feet. Annabel was gone. Passed away. Good golly, they had been about the same age. At thirty-five? No way. She was too young to die.

The lawyer placed his hand on the boy's shoulder, causing Adan's gaze to shift. He studied the boy. Gold eyes, just like Annabel. Had her same nose too, though it looked more boyish than cute on the kid. Darker hair. More brownish.

Kinda like…

Adan swallowed hard, having a feeling he knew where this was going.

"This is Jet Garrison. Annabel's son."

He yanked off his hat, setting it on the desk with a *thud*. "How—" His voice cracked like he was a teenager again. "How old?"

"Twelve, sir," the boy Jet answered.

Thirty-five minus twelve. Crud. For the love of everything. It couldn't be. Could it?

Adan would have been twenty-three at the heyday of his pro bull riding career. When the kid was born.

"You're… Adan Franco, right?" Jet asked.

He thought they'd established that fact already. "Yeah." He almost added *the famous bull rider*, but stopped himself. It was usually what came after the question with most folks. Though he got the distinct impression, it wasn't what the kid was gonna say.

"Mama said…" The boy's gold eyes glistened and rimmed with red. He straightened his back, frowning. "Mama said I can trust you."

Now why would the boy need to trust him?

"Mr. Franco," the attorney started. "According to Annabel Garrison's records, she lists you as… Um. The boy's father."

Adan actually felt all the blood rush from his head. His throat constricted and his vision narrowed. He ground his jaw shut, trying to regain control of his faculties. Wouldn't do no one any good if he lashed out. Or passed out.

Twenty-three when the kid was born. Nine months before that. He wished he could outright deny the possibility. But he couldn't. Though he didn't remember ever crossing that line with Annabel, he hadn't exactly been living the Christian life back then.

Should he ask for a DNA test? What would the kid do if he wasn't his dad? What would he do if he was? Adan scrubbed his hands over his face and beard. Then he shot to his feet, smashing his tan cowboy hat into place.

"Jet. You too old for a coloring book?"

The *duh* look on the kid's face confirmed exactly that.

"How about legos?"

"I like 'em."

"'Kay. There should be a box of legos over in the corner. Can I trust you to play with the legos while Mr. Haynes and I talk outside?"

"Yes, sir."

Jet slid off the chair and retrieved the box of legos. Adan waited for the boy to settle on the leather couch, dumping the contents of the legos onto the coffee table. Then Adan jerked his head toward the door indicating Mr. Haynes should proceed him. He closed the door behind him.

After walking into an empty stall not too far down the alleyway, Adan spoke.

"Look, I wasn't no saint back then, but I don't think I ever... You know... With Annabel. We were good friends. Nothing more."

"Are you asking for a paternity test?"

Was he?

"Maybe. I don't know. How positive was she? Did you ever talk to her?"

"Yes, in her last days, I spoke with Ms. Garrison. She listed your name on Jet's birth certificate."

Adan shook his head. "If she really believed I was, then why didn't she reach out? She knew me well enough to know I would have stepped up. Paid support. Visitation. Joint custody. If not marriage."

Haynes' shoulders lifted before a loud burst of air *whooshed* from his mouth. "We didn't discuss Jet's parentage other than for her to say she wanted you to raise him. When I found his birth certificate, I just assumed."

Adan lifted his cowboy hat and ran a hand through his hair before jamming it down again. Then he widened his stance and propped fisted hands on his hips.

"What happened to her?"

"Cancer."

The back of his eyes bit as he pictured poor sweet Annabel wasting from the disease. Had the kid watched it unfold? If so, he probably ought to get him into counseling.

Wait a minute. Was he actually thinking he'd step up for a kid that probably wasn't even his own?

Haynes cleared his throat again, a sound that was starting to grate on Adan's last nerve. "She asked me to give you this."

The attorney pulled a thick envelope from the inside of his suit jacket before handing it to Adan. He accepted it, seeing it as symbolic for assuming the guardianship of her son. He still didn't think the kid was his.

"So what's next?" he asked, even though he wasn't sure he wanted to know.

"Since your name is on his birth certificate, not much. As far as the law is concerned, you're his father. Unless you want to contest it."

"If I don't now, but decide to later, can I?"

"Mr. Franco, may I be candid?"

Wasn't he already?

"Please."

"If you don't think he's your son and want to pursue a paternity test, then I will need to take him to Child Services."

Well, crud. He couldn't let that happen. Not when Annabel told the kid he could trust him. 'Sides, he had the means to take care of Jet, though it meant the next few days required him to figure out a whole heap of things. First and foremost where they'd live. 'Cause no way was the kid gonna stay in the bunkhouse. Way too young for that, no matter how tame most of the Vargas cowboys appeared.

"I'll take care of him. So, no other legal paperwork is needed?"

"Not for you to take guardianship of your son."

It all seemed too bizarre for it to be that easy.

"She had some assets she wanted to leave for Jet and his guardian. And if you want, you can travel to Albuquerque to go through their things. Decide what to pack up and move and what to get rid of. If you don't, then there are funds in the estate for me to see to it. Though, I think it would be best for the boy to choose a few things of hers as keepsakes."

"I need to make some arrangements before that will be possible."

"Any questions, Mr. Franco?"

"Only a million," he said, thumping a fisted hand against the side of his leg. "But no, none for you. Thank you, Mr. Haynes."

"Here's my card. I'm based out of Albuquerque and will be headed back tonight. Call any time. If you decide to travel to their house, let me know and I can meet you to let you in."

"Yeah, thanks. I'll let you know soon."

"Good day, Mr. Franco."

Adan made sure the attorney could find his way out of the stables before he headed back to Dylan's office. Right outside, he mentally slapped a palm to his forehead. He was supposed to lead a trail ride for the resort guests. He texted Dylan, who responded that he asked Parker to take over. Good.

Then Adan texted back, *Gonna need a week or so off. Got to get my son settled.*

It half surprised him when Dylan responded with a simple, *take what you need.* They were too old of friends for Dylan not to say something about it. Maybe his friend decided they'd catch up later.

As Adan eased open the door to Dylan's office, Jet looked up. His heart about tore in two over the sadness and fear in the kid's eyes. Adan strode over and kneeled in front of him. The popping sound in his knee reminded him not to stay like that for too long.

"Looks like it's you and me, bud."

"Are you really my dad?"

"Seems like it."

Even if he wasn't, he had decided in that empty stall to take on the responsibility. Kid wouldn't understand the nuance of DNA tests. Nor would test results provide the best life for him. No, the moment he stepped up to the challenge, he became the kid's dad for better or worse, regardless of blood ties.

Lord, I'm gonna need a heap of help with this one.

He glanced at his watch. Three-thirty. He could leave Jet at the children's center until five. Give him time to pack up his things and call his parents. Figured at least for the time being, he'd move back home. Yeah, at thirty-five. With a kid in tow. Mama was gonna have a fit to be sure.

SOLANA VARGAS FELT a little bad she hadn't sent Adan a warning text. They were, after all, friends. Close friends. Friends when she wanted so much more.

She sighed as she watched the attorney climb behind the wheel of his sedan. He asked if he could leave the boy's things in the office and if she would kindly let Mr. Franco know, right after letting it slip that the boy was Adan's.

Her stomach knotted as tight as a spool of fence wire. Adan had a son. That changed everything. At least everything for Adan. And the rumor would spread like wildfire through the ranch staff. The perfect Christian man, former pro bull rider, had a son, without being married. It was the complete opposite of the Adan she knew.

Solana allowed the shock to wash over her. For some reason, she still believed him to be a godly man. One look at the kid and it was clear, if Adan had really fathered him, it had been during his pro bull riding career nearly a lifetime ago.

She still remembered watching him on TV, thinking no man could ever be as gorgeous as him. At twelve years old, she sported a major crush on him — one that had faded as she matured into adulthood. Then he came back to Vargas Ranch ten years ago, during her junior year of high school. She worked in the dining hall in the evenings back then. It was before she worked in the office. The moment she saw him, the crush came back.

Standing, Solana walked over to the boy's things and moved them behind her desk, out of view of the guests. Now she worked at the front desk at the resort, going on six years. Adan came in often, chatting with her each time. They had struck up a friendship and her crush changed to that of a grown woman falling for a man.

Unfortunately, Adan Franco saw her as his best friend's little cousin. A girl who had followed him around during the off season, asking a million questions about being a famous pro bull rider. Solana had tried many times over the past five years to get him to see her as a woman. Nothing she did worked, not even the one dance they shared at her cousin's wedding.

So, yeah, she may have been thinking about that a little when the attorney first appeared asking about him. Then again, what would she have texted Adan, anyway? *There's a man with a boy that I think he's gonna say is your son?*

Solana sighed as she flopped onto her office chair.

"That's an awful lot of sighing out there," her older sister Renata said from her office before she appeared in the doorway. "What's going on?"

"Not my story to tell."

"Your sighs tell me otherwise. Whose bags?"

Renata studied them for a second, and probably guessed they belonged to a kid.

Adan burst through the door. "Oh, good. You're here."

Solana straightened. That little hitch in her chest ached — the same one she got every time she saw him in loose denim with the large oval belt buckle and his tan cowboy hat. Only this time, worry and stress etched his handsome face.

"I don't know how to ease into this," he said. "So… I have a… Jet is…"

"Your son," Solana finished for him, hoping her saying it helped him in some small way. If nothing else, it eased her toward accepting it. She shoved away the mix of feelings it churned inside of her.

Adan's eyes rounded. "How'd you know?"

"The attorney dropped off his things." She hooked a thumb over her shoulder toward the black luggage.

"Oh."

Adan rubbed a hand on the back of his neck. "Lanni, I could really use —"

"My help? Anything." Solana's voice sounded far more supportive than she felt, despite his tender use of her nickname. Normally, it caused her insides to go gooey and she would bend over backwards to help him.

Adan's head angled to the side, much like Dalton's dog did when she was confused.

"Raina said she'd watch him until the children's center closes in like," he glanced at his watch, "an hour and fifteen. That's not enough time to figure out what to do."

"Adan, let's chat in Rennie's office while she watches the front desk."

"Um. Yeah. Great."

He spun around, nearly colliding with Renata, who quickly sidestepped him. Solana tossed her a thanks before ducking into her office.

"Tell me what you know."

Solana leaned against the edge of the desk while Adan paced the length of the room, relaying the events of the last half hour.

"I knew Jet's mother, Annabel, when I was on the PBR

circuit. We were good friends."

And he slept with her. She didn't have to hear the words to know it. A twinge of jealousy flared, which Solana rushed to tamp down. Wouldn't help the situation or cause him to see her as mature.

"Long story short, you have a son she never told you about. Until now."

"Until now... Lanni, she passed away. That boy watched his mama die from cancer."

Her shoulders sagged. Ugh. Now she regretted feeling jealous a minute ago. Poor Jet.

"She never contacted me about him, but I guess she put my name on the birth certificate. I don't..."

Solana waited, holding her breath. She could feel his anxiety in each stuttered step and clipped word as his boots clopped on the tile floor.

"I guess I need to go pack. Move out of the bunkhouse and take him to my parents." He paced the room, no longer looking at her. "Mama's gonna give me an earful."

"Adan. Deep breaths. Let's call your mama."

"Yeah. Yeah."

She had never seen him so upset.

He yanked his phone from his shirt pocket and it flew out of his hand, nearly smacking her in the face. She retrieved it from where it came to rest on the floor and handed it back.

"Sorry."

When she placed her hand on his forearm, he stilled, his blue eyes snapping to hers. Her breath lodged in her throat as sparks sizzled between them. At least for her, they always did. Judging by the storm in his eyes, she wondered if he felt it this time. She could only hope, even if now was the worst timing.

He shook his head as if to clear his mind; the moment gone. Then he mashed his thumb on the fingerprint reader and scrolled through his contacts. He pressed the dial button and held his phone to his ear.

"Mama. I'm gonna cut to the chase. One of my friends—
"

"Yes, female. From the pro circuit. She passed away. Says I'm her boy's father. He's here now."

"No, not here listening to this conversation. Here in Arizona. Can we stay with you until I can find a place?"

Solana listened to his side of the conversation, wishing he had put it on speaker so she could hear Heidi Franco's reaction. Then again, maybe it was better she couldn't.

"I'll pack up and be over in about an hour and a half."

"Sure. A late supper with you and Dad would be nice."

After Adan swiped the phone off, he turned toward her.

"You think you could watch him if I'm not back here in thirty?"

"I can come help you pack."

He eyed her warily.

Taking matters into her own hands, Solana grabbed his calloused hand, deposited her black cowgirl hat on her head, and led him out to his truck. She climbed into the passenger seat, not giving him a chance to refuse. He sighed heavily, much like she had earlier, before driving them over to the bunkhouse.

It only took them thirty minutes to stuff his clothes into a few suitcases and box up his books and personal items. Seemed insignificant for a thirty-five-year-old man who had won big in the rodeo. She figured all his buckles and such must be in storage or at his parents' place in town.

On the way back to the resort, Adan dropped another bomb.

"Looks like I'll need to head over to Albuquerque in a few days to pack up Jet's things. Maybe some mementos from his mom."

Solana remembered how hard it had been when she helped Aunt Catalina go through her grandfather's things almost two years ago. Her stomach clenched over the memory.

"How am I gonna figure out what to keep for him? Where are we gonna live? How am I gonna be a dad to a twelve-year-old boy who watched his mama die?"

"Adan, breathe. You've got this. God will provide everything you need. You know this."

He jammed the shifter into Park, hands flailing into his lap. The defeated set of his jaw, his rounded shoulders, and the lost look in his eyes had words flying from her mouth before she thought them through.

"I'll go to Albuquerque with you."

His eyes formed giant saucers as his head swiveled toward her. "Come again?"

"I have some vacation time saved up. A ton actually." She huffed. "I'll go with you and Jet to help."

"You can't take time off. It's the beginning of October. You know, peak season."

"I can and I will. Rennie lets other employees take time off during peak season. Just not too many at a time. Besides, we just hired another person for the front desk so I could start learning more of Rennie's job. She can train the new person, and I'll pick up my additional responsibilities when I get back."

"I don't know. What'll your parents think?"

"Adan Franco, you have enough to worry about. I can handle my family. And," lest he forget, though she wouldn't say that aloud, "I'm a grown woman and I've decided you need my help. Besides, I can't think of a better way to spend my vacation."

"You sure?"

"Yeah."

Adan expelled a gusty breath, relief written all over his face. "You are a godsend, Solana."

Or a complete idiot, she thought. Too late to back out now.

2

———————

ADAN DROPPED SOLANA off at the resort office, grabbing Jet's suitcases on the way out of the building. He tossed them in the back seat of his extended cab truck. Then he hurried to the children's center to pick up the boy. He snatched the envelope from the attorney off the center console before stuffing it inside. He'd go through that later. Much later.

"My parents live in Wickenburg. That's the closest big town. About thirty minutes from here."

Jet stared out the side window, giving no sign he heard.

"They have a nice three-bedroom home. We'll stay there until I can get us a place."

Jet snorted.

"What?"

"You don't have a house?"

Adan pulled onto the paved freeway, resisting the temptation to stretch his neck muscles. The tension corded them tightly, causing his head to throb.

"No. I'm a single wrangler at Vargas Ranch. Never had much need for a big old house." An empty house to taunt him about his inability to find a wife and settle down? No, thank you.

"You're old."

Adan counted to ten and shot up a prayer for patience, forcing himself to remember the kid had been through a lot. If the disrespect continued, he'd have words with him.

"My mama's name is Heidi. And my dad's name is Harley. You'll call them Ms. Heidi and Mr. Harley. Understood?"

From the corner of his eye, Adan saw Jet's single shoulder shrug. Guess that meant "yes."

The hum of the tires against the hot asphalt reverberated through the cab of his truck. He considered playing some music, but too many thoughts spun in his mind.

His stomach tightened. Mama would be disappointed in him. He never told his parents about how far he'd fallen in his pro bull riding days. Though he figured Mama had suspected he'd been no saint back then. Still, Jet was breathing proof he hadn't been living out his faith like he should have.

Adan expelled a puff of air, catching himself at the last minute, quick enough to keep it from sounding too loud. They had welcomed his younger sister, Brisa, and her disabled son with open arms. Surely, they'd do the same for Jet.

"Why can't we live in my house?"

Jet's words knifed Adan. The innocent, yet logical, question further highlighted the kid's losses.

"My job is here. So we'll get a place in the area. Wickenburg or Forepaugh."

"But all my friends are in Albuquerque."

"Jet, I live here and have a life here. My job is here."

Jet grunted and folded his arms over his chest. Adan hated to rip the boy away from the life he had known, but he had no mind to move away from his family. He would need all the help he could get raising a preteen.

He shook his head as he exited the two-lane highway. Still couldn't believe Solana volunteered to go with him to deal with Annabel's house. He should bring Jet with him. Give the boy a chance for some closure as they packed up the house, no matter how difficult it would be.

Besides Dylan, Solana was his best friend. She understood him and encouraged him. And she was his heart's desire. Too bad she was so young. The age difference between them spanned a decade. As if that hadn't been enough to deter him from pursuing a relationship with her, his new single dad status had to be the proverbial nail in that coffin. No twenty-five-year-old woman wanted to take on a long-time thirty-five-year-old bachelor with a twelve-year-old son. Good grief, she could almost split the difference between his age and Jet's. The thought settled on his stomach like a boulder. All they could ever be was friends.

Adan blinked. He had turned onto his parents' street without realizing it. He pulled along the curb in front of the quaint stucco house he'd called home for the first eighteen years of his life. As soon as possible, he'd do his best to get him and Jet a place. Wasn't fair to his parents, especially with Dad retiring in a few months.

The door of the house opened as he cut the engine. His parents hovered in the doorway. When Dad glanced at the back of the truck, he descended the stairs.

When Jet grumbled, an admonition to mind his manners died on the tip of Adan's tongue. Getting to know him ought to come before too much nagging.

Jet eased the truck door open, but not before Adan noticed his trepidation. Yeah, he must remember the kid had been through a lot. This couldn't be easy for him.

"You must be Jet," Dad said, holding the door while the boy slid out.

"Yes, sir."

"Harley's fine."

"Mr. Harley."

Jet ducked his head and stepped around Dad before he closed the door. Then he scuffed toward the sidewalk.

Dad caught Adan's attention and raised an eyebrow. Adan circled his truck and hugged his dad.

"Can you help me unload?" he asked.

"Sure thing, son."

Adan grabbed Jet's suitcases out of the extended cab before handing them to Jet. "Go greet my mama and then take these inside."

"Yes, sir."

Good. At least he found his manners without Adan prompting him.

Adan dropped the tailgate on his truck and slid a heavy box to the edge. When Dad started to reach for it, he suggested the suitcases for him while Adan carried the box.

Once inside, Adan climbed the stairs to his old bedroom, stomach sinking with each step. It felt plain weird to move back home at his age. Didn't like it.

Mama kissed his cheek in passing. "I fixed up Brisa's old room for Jet. Sorry for the color and frilly touches."

"Thank you, Ms. Heidi," Jet murmured before dropping his suitcases just inside the door.

Adan set the box on the floor near the window of his room. Then he pivoted to head back out to the truck. He glimpsed Brisa's room and cringed. Poor Jet. Wasn't an ounce of masculinity present in the room.

"Jet, you need help unpacking?" Mama asked.

"No, ma'am."

"Alright. When you've finished, come on down to the kitchen. You can tell me more about yourself while I finish making supper."

"Yes, Ms. Heidi."

Adan breathed a little easier as he bounded down the stairs. Dad followed behind him to finish unloading the truck.

"So... A son?"

"Guess so. The lawyer says I'm listed as his dad on his birth certificate."

"Hmm."

"What I don't get is why his mama didn't tell me years ago. I might not remember... I'm not one hundred percent sure he's mine. If he was, why didn't Annabel let me know? I would have been involved in his life years ago."

"You said she died?"

"Yeah. Cancer." He scarcely believed it. "We had been close friends back in my rodeo circuit days. I just don't remember crossing any lines with her. Some other women? Sure. Not proud of it. But Annabel? No."

"Are you gonna contest it?"

"And leave him to the foster system? With my name on his birth certificate? Not a chance. There's got to be a good reason she put my name on it."

Dad squeezed his shoulder. "We'll talk more later. Your mother already pulled up a few listings in Forepaugh and the northwest part of town."

Adan snorted. "Yikes?"

Dad laughed. "She knows you. You're welcome to stay as long as you need. But she figured you wouldn't want to stay long."

"Yeah."

Adan balanced the last box against the rim of the truck bed while he flipped the tailgate closed. Then he carried the box to his room before joining the rest of the family in the dining room.

Mama and Jet set the table while Dad poured drinks. He took his usual seat across from Mama. Jet sat to his left.

Dad offered a pleasant prayer, and Adan quieted his mind long enough to hear it. He said a silent prayer of his own for wisdom and guidance.

Mama, clearly great with kids, asked Jet about himself throughout the meal. Adan listened, almost wishing he could take notes so he would forget nothing. He wanted to be a wonderful dad, even if he had been unprepared for it.

"I enjoy riding horses," Jet said. "Mama used to take me before... She got too sick."

"Was there a stable nearby?" Mama asked.

"Yeah. We boarded our horses there."

Crud. Adan figured he'd have to haul them back to Vargas Ranch with him.

"What's your horse's name?" he asked Jet.

"Optimus Prime. I usually call him Optimus."

Adan and Dad chuckled at the same time. Adan held out his fist for a bump.

"Nice name."

Jet tapped his fist before he shrugged. Then he chewed a bite of mac-n-cheese, a small smile twitching at the corner of his mouth.

Adan would ask the attorney about Annabel's horses just in case they didn't own them. He didn't want to cause more pain for the boy.

When supper concluded, he stood and placed his large hand on Jet's slim shoulder. Swallowing back a sudden rush of emotion, he asked Jet to finish unpacking. Mama volunteered to help and to show him around the house.

Then Adan grabbed a stack of dishes and silverware, carrying them into the kitchen. From as far back as he could remember, Dad and he handled dishes. Sometimes Brisa helped, if she hadn't cooked the meal with Mama.

He coughed as he set the stack on the counter near the dishwasher. He ran a hand over his face and beard. Reality caught up to him and he murmured, "I'm a father. A father of a young man in the making. Who lost his mama. His home. Everything."

Tears moistened his cheeks as he leaned against the bar. His dad stood in front of him, hands resting on his shoulders. He looked up and held Adan's gaze.

"Yeah. You are." Dad cleared his throat. "No man is ready for the moment he becomes a father. And the way God allowed you to become a dad? Well, it's a shock." Dad squeezed his shoulders. "Adan, one thing I know, God has a plan for you and for that hurting boy. And He isn't gonna leave you to do it on your own. He'll be right there with you every step of the way."

Adan's eyes darted to the corner of the room. He knew that. Had counseled the same to many friends, cowboys, and even the male athletes in the Vargas Sports Bible study. But he'd never faced such a massive challenge in his life. He felt so inadequate. Uncertain. Lost.

"Son, your mother and I are here for you. So are your sister and Dylan and the entire Vargas clan. We will all walk beside you, too."

Adan straightened his shoulders, sucking in a long breath. Just because he couldn't feel God's presence didn't mean He wasn't working in his life.

On a shaky breath, he said, "Those dishes ain't gonna wash themselves."

Dad scoffed. "No, they won't. Come here."

Then his dad wrapped him in a comforting embrace, followed by a few pats on the back and another squeeze of his shoulder. Adan nodded, acknowledging the unspoken challenge of his heart. He could do this. Would do this with God's help.

ONCE BACK IN the front office, Solana texted her mom. *Need to talk. Mind if I stop by after supper?*

Three little dots danced while Mom typed back a response. *Come for supper. I haven't started it yet. Bring Rennie.*

Solana: *Be there at 5:30?*

Mom: *See you soon!*

"You want to go home for supper?" she asked as she stood in the doorway of Renata's office.

Her older sister studied her face for several seconds, dark eyes softening. "I'd love to, but maybe another night. It seems you could use a good long talk with Mom."

Solana bit her lip. "You know me so well."

Rennie rounded her desk and hugged her. "You go. We'll catch up later."

"Thanks, Sis."

"Give Mom and Dad my love."

Solana waved her hand to acknowledge the comment before retrieving her purse and keys from her desk. Then she shut off her computer and turned off the desk lamp. She flipped the sign on the resort office window with the message to text Rennie's number for after hours check-ins or issues.

Then she headed out to her Jeep Cherokee. Sliding behind the wheel, she started it, flipping the AC on to take the edge off the heat that built up while it sat in the sun all day. Normally, she would play some loud music, singing along. Not on this drive. Too much churned inside of her, like a violent dust devil, whipping up dirt and debris, high into the sky. She could only hope the turmoil would be as fleeting.

Adan had a son.

Her shoulders drooped. Any hope she held out that he would finally notice her evaporated. It was so unfair. He would be very busy in the coming months or more. That heartbroken kid would need a mom. Adan would need a wife. Sure, lots of men were single dads. But, Adan? Couldn't he see he would need her?

A sob stuck in her throat as she turned onto the highway. She swallowed it down, trying to control her emotions and drive safely. She punched the AC button off and rolled down her windows, now that the interior of her car had cooled down. The fresh evening air helped bolster her resolve not to cry.

Maybe it was time to accept that she and Adan would only ever be friends. At twenty-five-years-old, she still had plenty of time to fall in love with someone else. Ross Braxton was cute enough. Cute? Really? Was she in high school or was she an adult?

No one could compare to Adan. The way his blue eyes lit up when he smiled at her. His laugh. Oh, how she loved it! It could breathe life back into a tough day. And his faith? Rock solid. An inspiration to everyone who met him. She couldn't picture herself with anyone else.

Thirty minutes later, she pulled off the highway and wound her way through Wickenburg to her parents' home — the same house she grew up in — no closer to figuring out her life. The light tan stucco ranch-style home sat on an acre of property on the outskirts of town.

She parked behind her dad's weathered truck. After rolling up the windows and cutting the engine, she sat there for a moment under the heaviness of her heart.

Solana finally exited her vehicle and walked up to the front door. She eased it open as she announced her presence.

"Hey, Lanni!" Her dad greeted her, stepping into the great room from his office. "Your mom ran out to get Chinese food since you girls were coming home."

She crossed the room to her dad, resting her head against his chest for an extra few seconds when he hugged her, allowing his comfort to soothe her heart.

"Where's Rennie?"

"She couldn't make it."

"Oh. Still glad to see you."

Dad's dark eyes studied her for a second. Solana bowed her head and shifted her gaze away.

"Uh, oh. What's wrong?"

She groaned before skulking into the kitchen. "Let's wait until Mom gets home. I don't feel like explaining it twice."

"Okay, mija. Whatever makes you happy."

Solana stifled a groan. What would make her happy? That'd be Adan's wedding ring on her finger and babies of their own. Not happening. The sooner she accepted it, the sooner she could move on with her life.

The low hum of the garage door sounded. Dad lingered by the door between the kitchen and garage. Solana grabbed three glasses from the cupboard and filled them with ice before pouring herself a soda. Then she filled Mom's with iced tea and left Dad's empty. He wasn't as predictable as Mom.

"Lanni! I'm so happy you came over tonight." Mom set the bag of Chinese food on the island as Dad grabbed a stack of paper plates. "No Rennie?"

She shook her head.

Dad said a blessing over the food before they closed the prayer with the Vargas family motto: "We do not deviate from the Lord's plan."

Solana huffed as she reached for a plate. If only she understood what God's plan was with Adan and her heart that he'd stolen years ago. And now his surprise son.

"What happened?" Mom asked.

Solana stuffed a fried potsticker in her mouth as she weighed what to say. While she chewed, she studied her parents. She favored her mom's appearance with her fair skin and slender build. Mom sported light brown hair, whereas Solana's matched her dad's black hair. She and her dad shared many similar facial features, though his caramel skin had been passed down only to Rennie. Other than that, Rennie looked like the latina version of their mom.

Her parents had been married for thirty years. They had shared a deep, unbreakable bond. She wanted a marriage like that. With Adan.

"An attorney came by the office today. Looking for Adan."

As Mom balanced noodles on her chopsticks, she glanced at Solana with eyes full of sympathy.

"With Adan's son."

"What?" Dad asked. "He has a son?"

"Twelve-year-old boy."

Dad pounded a fist against his chest. "That's a relief."

"Diego," Mom warned.

"Well, it is. I couldn't fathom him fooling around. Not with how devout he is. But, twelve? That'd be from his rodeo days."

Solana widened her eyes, trying to send her mom a message.

"Diego. Let Solana finish."

"Sorry, mija. Continue."

Solana gave the highlights, finishing with a rushed breath. "And I promised to go with him to Albuquerque to help close up his late-friend's house."

This earned her a deep scowl from her father and rounded eyes from her mother.

"Absolutely not," Dad said.

"Dad, I'm twenty-five. It's my decision. Besides, it's Adan. You have nothing to worry about."

"Do you hear yourself? Nothing to worry about? Bah," Dad grumbled. "Says my daughter about the man she loves who fathered a kid twelve years ago?"

Mom put a hand on Dad's forearm. He instantly pursed his lips.

Solana scooped up a forkful of fried rice, thinking through her response.

"First, we won't ever be alone. His son will be with us. Second, could you imagine trying to go through a late-friend's things by yourself? It's going to be hard. He needs someone to help."

Mom turned toward Dad, and the two of them seemed to communicate telepathically. It always weirded her out growing up. At last, Dad dipped his head, deferring to Mom.

"Lanni, are you sure you want to do this?"

Ugh. She hated when Mom went all soft and empathetic. It usually preceded some very sage advice—advice she wasn't sure she wanted to hear.

"Let me have it."

"It's just... We know you have feelings for him. We don't want to see you get hurt."

Dad snorted and Mom silenced him with a lightning quick look.

"We think it's admirable that you want to help him and—what is the boy's name?"

"Jet."

"Jet. But Adan has much to process. Becoming a dad.

Setting up a home. Helping Jet grieve. I would hate to see him take advantage of you."

"Mom, he would never do that."

Dad cleared his throat. "Maybe not physically. But emotionally. He won't even know he's doing it."

The sweet and sour chicken turned to sand in her mouth. She swallowed, chasing it with a gulp of soda. Dad and Mom said nothing more while they ate a few bites.

Solana considered their words. They were right that Adan would be vulnerable. She could be there for him. Let him lean on her. Finally prove to him she would make a great companion and helpmate. Maybe he would even see her as motherly and wifely. Was that even a word?

"Although..."

Solana's head snapped toward her mom.

"Having a woman's presence might ease the transition for both Adan and Jet."

Did her mom really just say that?

Dad retorted, "Then Heidi can go with them."

"Brisa depends on her for some of Braden's appointments," Solana said.

"Wouldn't hurt Dylan to take his son to physical therapy."

"He'll be short-staffed with Adan gone, so there's that," Solana added.

At last, Dad dropped his hands to his lap, rubbing his thighs. "I'm not even a little comfortable with this idea of yours."

She straightened her back and held his gaze. "I've heard you loud and clear, Dad, Mom. I appreciate your concern and will watch for what you've mentioned."

Dad sighed. "Sounds like you're still going on a road trip, though."

"If he wants my help, then yes."

After that, the conversation moved on to the family's feed store that Dad sold his share of Vargas Ranch to buy years ago. He and Mom loved working at the store, helping the locals and being an active part of the community. She knew Dad had wanted independence from his brother and parents.

So why couldn't he understand her desire to decide on her own? It was her life. Her friend. And she would do what she thought was right, with or without their blessing.

When they finished supper, Solana made a hasty retreat to her shared apartment in the women's dorms on the ranch, disappointed her parents failed to support her decision.

3

ADAN EASED ONTO the couch and rubbed his knee. Jet sat in the middle and Mama on the far end. Dad turned on a superhero movie, probably trying to appeal to the preteen.

As the movie started, Adan opened his laptop and pressed the power button before he donned a pair of drugstore readers. Maybe all those head injuries in his rodeo days contributed to the need for them. Mama had emailed him a few links to houses in the area, so he pulled up the first one. The curb appeal looked nice. A three bedroom single story in the next subdivision over from his parents. Kinda smaller than he envisioned.

His mind conjured an image of him, Jet, Solana, and a few little kids with silky black hair, just like hers. He raked a hand through his hair. Even if it was a fantasy, the thought gave him pause. Should he buy the house he wanted for the long-term now? Or buy something suitable for him and Jet, knowing he might sell it later?

"Jet, would you like to sit over here? You can see the movie better," Mama said.

"I guess."

Mama swapped seats with him before peering over Adan's shoulder. Keeping her voice low, she asked, "What's bothering you?"

"Do I get a house with the future in mind or something that works for us now?"

"Well... It depends. Do you think you'll marry soon?"

Adan snorted. "Been trying to find someone for a long time, Mama."

"Oh, I know. I just..." Mama shook her head. "If you buy a house and you marry later, there's always a chance your future wife won't care for it and will want something else."

Adan's stomach clenched, right along with his jaw. He hadn't considered that.

"Of course, any house you buy you can always sell. So it's really up to you."

Dad cleared his throat and jerked his head toward the movie, annoyance written on his face.

"Let's talk in the dining room."

Adan followed his mother, carrying his laptop in one hand and a soda in the other. When he plunked his things on the table, she continued.

"Do you want horse property? A small, low maintenance yard?"

He groaned. "I don't know. I hadn't planned on any of this. Haven't given a house any thought."

"What about renting for now?"

He rubbed a hand over his beard. "What about lost equity?"

"If you rent for six months or even a year, that will give you time to think about what you want."

That earlier image played in his mind's eye again. A kid needed a yard to play in. Jet owned a horse. Probably would bring back Annabel's too. And Adan owned one. Though, he enjoyed riding Trixie Wind for trail rides at Vargas Ranch and had no desire to shuttle her back and forth every day.

"Keep in mind that you aren't likely to move in to anything for thirty days, especially if it is owner occupied. Unless you plan to offer cash?"

Adan's shoulders bunched. He had not thought of that either. He needed to call his investment advisor first thing tomorrow to withdraw the funds for a house. His rodeo winnings and endorsements over the years set him up with a solid financial footing. And working at the ranch where virtually every expense was included helped, too.

"Hey." Dad stuck his head in the dining room. "Looks like someone is ready for bed."

"Thanks. Guess I'll go figure that out."

Mama squeezed his hand. "You don't have to solve everything tonight. And like we said, you're welcome to stay here as long as you need."

"Thanks, Mama."

Adan snapped his laptop shut and tucked it under his arm before he tossed his soda can in the recyclables. He hooked the readers on the edge of his shirt. Then he nudged Jet.

"Time for bed, bud."

Jet stretched and took his sweet time standing. He trudged up the stairs in front of Adan, whining as if the effort equaled climbing a mountain.

"Why don't you put your pjs on and I'll come in to pray with you in a minute?"

Jet stepped back. "You would do that?"

"'Course."

"Mama always did that."

Adan ruffled the kid's hair and flashed him a sympathetic smile. Then he closed Jet's bedroom door before he entered his room. He plugged in his laptop next to his bed, intending to view more houses online after he prayed with Jet. Then he dropped his phone on its quick charger.

When he walked back to Jet's room, he turned his ear toward the door. Hearing no sounds, he knocked. A soft grunt replied, so he opened the door. Jet sat on the bed, his back against the headboard, wearing a soft t-shirt and loose shorts.

Adan's head throbbed. The kid would be a teenager before he knew it. Then a man. He only had a few years to speak into his life. The weightiness of the responsibility felt so tangible he could almost see it.

He rounded to the far side of the bed and eased onto the edge, crooking his good knee on the top so he could angle toward Jet.

"I know the last while has been tough for you. And you and I are just getting to know each other." Adan paused, desperate to set a positive tone for their relationship. "I want you to know I will always be here for you. It's you and me from here on out."

Jet's eyes watered, and his chin dipped to his chest.

"Hey," Adan said, jiggling the boy's lower leg. "It's gonna be alright. We'll go back to Albuquerque and pack up your things. Pick up your horse. Find a place to live."

Jet sniffed and Adan's heart just plain hurt for him.

"Six days from now will be a little better than today. And six weeks a little better than six days. And in six months, when we've settled into a routine again, you know what?"

Jet shook his head.

"You'll look back on all this and think about how you thought you could never make it through this. But you did. And we're gonna pray together every night. Ask God to help us through it. You hear me?"

"Yes, sir."

Adan jiggled his leg again.

"You can call me Adan, if you want."

"Okay, Adan."

"Anything you want me to pray for?"

Jet shrugged, so Adan bowed his head and let the Spirit lead him.

"Lord Jesus, we don't know why You brought me and Jet together. But we know You promise to never leave or forsake us. I ask for Your wisdom and discernment as I make the dozens of decisions I need to so we can get settled. And I ask that you comfort Jet in his loss. Help me, my family, and friends be Your hands and feet for Jet. In Jesus' name.

Amen."

When Adan looked up and saw Jet's shoulders shaking, he rounded the bed and pulled Jet into his arms. It seemed the most natural thing in the world to rock him back and forth as he clung to him, his own tears dampening his face before his beard swallowed them.

After a minute, Jet leaned back so Adan released him. Jet brushed his face against his arm, looking away.

"It's okay to cry sometimes," Adan whispered as he swiped the back of his hand over his cheeks.

Then he stood and flicked off the lights.

"Night, Jet."

"Night."

Once in the solitude of his room, Adan closed the door. He changed into his gym shorts and a t-shirt before propping the pillows up behind him on his bed. He placed his computer on his lap.

His childhood room felt foreign—just as foreign as the life he woke up to that morning. He started the day as a wrangler living in a bunkhouse and ended it as a single dad living in his parents' home.

Lord, I recognize nothing about my life. His prayer slammed into his heart. That had to be one of the many things Jet felt, too. *I need Your guidance and wisdom here.*

A text pinged on his phone from Solana. *How are you doing?*

He responded: *Can I call?*

His phone rang, and he answered it immediately.

"I have no clue what I'm doing."

Solana half laughed. "I'm not surprised."

"Do I buy a house? Rent a place? Buy a forever home? Buy a home short-term? What kind of property do I need? I don't own any furniture."

"Adan, slow down. Why do you have to buy or rent or decide tonight?"

He raked a hand through his hair as he stared at Solana's lovely face on his phone. Her dark eyes radiated empathy and her silky waves rested over one shoulder. He loved the way they often jumped into the middle of a conversation without missing a beat.

"You want me to come over?"

Though it sounded like what he needed, he shook his head. She couldn't see him as boyfriend material, not with him being a decade older than her. She was only being nice.

At last, he finally answered, "Naw. It's getting late."

She offered him a small smile.

"You're right. I guess I don't have to decide any of that tonight."

"Exactly. Why don't you spend the day at your parents' house tomorrow? I can come over and help you with a plan. We can call that attorney to see how soon we can drive out to Albuquerque."

"Yeah. Thanks, Lanni. That sounds pretty smart."

"You know you're the pretty one. I'm the smart one."

Adan chuckled at her joke, even though he thought she was both pretty and smart.

"Alright. See you in the morning."

"Solana?"

"Yeah?"

"Thanks."

His phone screen faded to black. She was right. He didn't have to figure it all out tonight or alone. And calling the attorney in the morning made sense. The sooner they made the trip to Albuquerque, the sooner Jet could settle in.

THE NEXT MORNING, Solana hurried through her morning routine. She apologized a dozen more times to Rennie, who scolded her to stop. She reminded her she could take vacation whenever she wanted and they would work around it.

She stopped at the coffee shop and picked up a black coffee for Adan and a pumpkin latte for herself. Then she drove into town, allowing the GPS to guide her. Even though she had known the Francos all her life, she had never been to their home. They always came over to Aunt Catalina's house on the ranch. Of course, with six thousand square feet of space, it made sense to host large extended family gatherings there.

Solana rolled her lips inward, a nervous habit when she became anxious or pensive. Adan wasn't her family. Sure felt like it, since he and Dylan had been friends forever. And Dylan married Adan's sister Brisa. And Dylan was Solana's cousin. So, it seemed she had spent many family dinners at her aunt and uncle's with Adan.

Ugh. Would she ever be able to let go of her desire for something more than friendship with him?

Maybe Dad was right. She should guard her heart—the impulsive one that got her into this weird mess.

Solana sighed and pushed open her SUV's door. She promised to help Adan today and in Albuquerque. If nothing else, she was a woman of her word.

Before she trudged up the porch stairs, the door flew open.

"Solana!" Heidi Franco greeted her warmly, easing her fears. "I'm so glad you are helping Adan."

Huh? Guess Heidi felt different from Dad and Mom.

"He really needs his friends right now."

"Glad to help." Somehow she managed to keep it from sounding like a question, which is how she heard the words in her mind.

"Brought a coffee for him."

"How thoughtful. Come on in."

Solana walked past Heidi and immediately caught sight of Adan in the dining room. He grinned and pushed back from the table, headed her way, propping his readers on the top of his head. Yeah, lifting his spirits was why she volunteered to help.

"For me?" Adan asked as he accepted the still warm coffee from her with one hand while wrapping his other arm around her for a hug.

Heat flooded her face at the contact. If he only knew how much she loved the scent of his bodywash, as she discovered the source while helping him pack. She used to think it was cologne. That musky, rich smell sent her pulse thrumming.

"I'm set up in here. But come meet Jet first. I should probably have him in school, but Mama thought it'd be better to wait until after we get back from New Mexico."

"Makes sense."

"Jet? Come meet my friend, Solana. She's going on our road trip to help."

"Hi, Jet," she said.

"Hi, Miss Solana."

"What kind of snacks do you like?"

"Um. BBQ chips, Krispie squares, and mocha fraps."

"Perfect. Water okay, too?"

He hitched his shoulder. "Sure."

When Jet shrank back against the couch cushion, Adan motioned her into the dining room.

"I figured we would start with the attorney."

"Sure, Adan. That makes sense."

As Solana sat next to him at the table, she took in the two-tone walls. White wainscotting along the bottom third complemented the bright yellow on the top. An ornate china cabinet stood behind the head of the table, proudly displaying a fine six-piece place setting with violets in the traditional purple and yellow.

Adan's phone beeped with each number he pressed. The line rang twice before the attorney's secretary answered, placing them on a brief hold until Mr. Haynes answered.

"It's Adan Franco. I have my friend Solana listening in. She's coming with us to clear out the Garrison house."

"When did you hope to leave?"

Adan raised a brow in her direction.

"I can leave whenever works for you."

"Tomorrow morning, okay?"

"Yeah."

"We'll be there tomorrow," Adan said to Mr. Haynes.

"Perfect. My wife will stock the fridge with some necessities. Just text my cell when you hit the city limits and I can meet you there."

Adan cleared his throat. "About the horses." He moved into the kitchen and lowered his voice. Solana could still hear, but she figured he was trying to spare Jet overhearing.

"Did they own Optimus Prime?"

The sound of mouse clicks came across the speaker. "Looks like they owned that horse and another, older horse. Silver Streak."

Adan gripped the counter in the kitchen as the color drained from his face.

"What is it?" she asked as she stood and moved closer.

"That was her barrel racing horse."

"She must be, what nineteen then?"

"Says here she's... Yes, you're correct. Nineteen," Mr. Haynes answered.

"She in good health?" Adan asked.

They discussed more specifics. Both horses were in good health and were boarded at a nearby ranch. Solana typed the name, address, and number of the ranch along with the address for the Garrison's house into her phone when the attorney rattled them off.

When Adan hung up, they both sat at the table again.

"How long does it take to go through someone's things?" Adan muttered as he rubbed a hand down his face and over his beard.

Solana's heart clenched. She hated the haunted look in his eyes and wished she could do more to help him.

"I don't know. Can we stay there?"

"I think so. Haynes said it's a three-bedroom, two bath place with an attached garage."

Adan's mom interjected, "Might be best to give yourself at least a week. Depending on how much they had and what you want to keep, it could take that long. Maybe longer."

Solana watched as he rubbed his temple with one hand. She clasped the other, offering what comfort she could through the friendly touch. When his eyes met her gaze, her breath hitched. He said so much with those blue eyes. Everything from "thank you" to "I couldn't do this without you" all without uttering a sound.

Suddenly, she realized that was exactly what she witnessed her parents do countless times. Both joy and sorrow blended in a bittersweet mix in her heart. Joy that she knew Adan so well she understood his unspoken words. Sorrow that she held out little hope of them forming a deeper relationship, despite her longing for more.

"Alright," she said, sliding his notepad toward her. "Two-horse trailer. I'll text Dylan to see if we can borrow one. What else?"

Adan shook his head. "I don't know. I guess we could research moving companies to ship the household goods. Even hauling the horse trailer, we'll have some room in the truck bed and the storage area of the trailer for a few things."

"Should we both drive?"

"No. I don't want you to put the wear and tear on your Cherokee."

"I can if we need the extra space."

"I'll hire movers. Just don't pack too heavy for the trip. You know, just one curling iron instead of two."

When his face split into a bright grin, Solana laughed.

"And here I thought I could bring all three."

Adan's chuckle eased the tension in the room. His mom smiled at his teasing before flashing her a thoughtful look. Unfortunately, Solana couldn't read Heidi's expressions like she could Adan's.

They spent the next hour planning what they needed to take with them and what to do before leaving in the morning.

"I can ask Dylan to hook up the horse trailer to my Cherokee. And I'll stay overnight at my parents' house so we can leave first thing."

"Yeah. That'd be great. Do you want us to pick you up over there?"

Solana glanced at Heidi. "Would you mind keeping an eye on my car?"

"Not at all. You can park it on the street here. I can drive it to the grocery store if you're worried about it sitting too long."

"Sounds like a plan. Adan, I'll be here by five-thirty. We can drop the trailer and hitch it to your truck. That will save us at least an hour or more."

The keys on his laptop clicked softly. "Looks like Maps shows driving back toward Phoenix to the 74 to I-17 to I-40 as the fastest route."

"We shouldn't hit rush hour, right?" she asked.

Adan shrugged. "Dunno."

Her phone pinged with a text from Madison, her cousin Derin's wife. Solana read it aloud.

"Madison said when they moved her things down from Colorado, the moving company stored her things for a reasonable fee. Might work for you if you aren't ready to receive it for a while."

"That's great. Ask her—"

"Got the name and a link to their website." Solana forwarded the text to Adan.

"Thanks. I'll make some calls."

"What else can I help with?"

Adan flashed his cheeseburger grin. "Road snacks? Breakfast tomorrow?"

"I'll handle both."

Solana stood and tucked her phone in her back pocket. Adan followed her to the front door after she spoke with Jet for a few minutes. He grasped her hand, and she looked into his eyes, her heart ever hopeful.

"I can't thank you enough for doing this. It means a lot, Lanni. Really, it's a tremendous weight off my shoulders just knowing you'll be with us."

"Happy to help."

He held her gaze for several seconds before he squeezed her hand. Then he released it and opened the door.

"I'm serious. Only one curling iron."

"Only if you limit yourself to one champion belt buckle."

"You know I have a separate suitcase just for them, right?"

Solana laughed all the way to her car. She had half a mind to pack a second curling iron as a joke. Before she pulled away, she waved to him, so very glad for the opportunity to support him through a tough season.

4

THE NEXT MORNING, Adan still chewed over Jet's comment after Solana left yesterday. *She your girlfriend?* He quickly denied it, but figured Jet believed him about as much as Mama did — which was not at all. In fact, Mama gave him a little warning to treat Solana well and to remember his faith.

Adan sighed as he unhitched the horse trailer from Solana's Cherokee. He tapped his knuckles against the back of her vehicle twice, letting her know it was safe to pull away.

As he stalked toward his truck, he held back a growl. Mama meant he should keep his hands to himself. Never had she doled out a warning like that before. Jet's existence already weakened Mama's trust. He hated it.

Still, he respected his parents and would be mindful of his actions with Solana and around his son. Besides, he doubted she harbored any secret romantic feelings for him. They were just friends.

He climbed behind the wheel of his truck and backed it up to the trailer. Solana secured the hitch and connected the wires. He cut the engine to double check it. Sure, he knew she probably did it right. Didn't matter, he and Dylan always checked each other on things like that. Safety first.

"Ready?" he asked.

"Yeah," she said, wheeling her suitcase behind her.

Adan took it from her. "Better be only one curling iron in this thing."

Solana was so beautiful with her black cowgirl hat, fancy denim pants, and flowing blouse. Feminine and confident. She flashed an impish grin, causing his heart to jump and his pulse to thrum. Maybe Mama's warning was warranted after all.

Once Adan stowed her luggage in the truck bed along with his and Jet's, he covered it with the foldable tonneau cover. He locked it before climbing into the cab.

Glancing over his shoulder, he confirmed Jet had buckled his seatbelt. Then he offered a prayer for safe travels. Waving to his parents, he eased away from the curb.

"Music?" Solana asked.

"Sure."

She punched on his satellite radio and chose their favorite country station, turning the volume down low. When he glanced in the rearview, he caught Jet's head lolling to the side.

"Must be nice to sleep through anything," Adan muttered.

"Already?" Solana asked.

He nodded.

She tapped the top of a paper coffee cup he hadn't noticed before. "I brought you a coffee."

"Bless you."

He swallowed a huge gulp, grateful for the caffeine. He hadn't slept well since becoming a father. Well, that sounded odd. Guess he'd been a father for twelve years and not known it.

That niggling feeling wrapped around his mind. He still couldn't remember anything more than a friendly hug from Annabel. Surely, if they'd been intimate, he would remember, right?

Solana's sweet voice sang the words along with the music, calming his inner turmoil. Adan wished he could share his doubts with her. Only, he couldn't risk Jet accidentally overhearing him. The last thing he wanted was to cause the tweener more distress. Best if Jet never knew about his doubts.

"What is it?"

Adan shook his head.

"I can see something is bothering you," Solana said.

"There is but..." He jerked his head toward the back seat.

"Okay. Maybe we can find time to talk about it later?"

"Yeah. Thanks."

The steady hum of his tires against the asphalt filled the cab, along with the soft sound of a country song about a man losing his girl. Adan punched the button to switch to a Christian station, needing to steer clear of love songs, since his heart sat in the seat next to him with her dark eyes and soft, wavy hair.

When they neared highway 74, they hit some traffic until they merged onto I-17 northbound.

"Good thing we aren't going that way," Solana said about the traffic headed into Phoenix. "We should try to time our trip back to avoid that traffic."

Adan didn't respond. Too many thoughts whirled in his mind. Having the next eight hours or so to ponder things might just drive him crazy.

"Tell me about your dream house," he blurted out.

"Um. Uh."

He glanced over at Solana in time to notice the pink on her cheeks before she stared out the side window.

"Come on," he said. "I'm sure you've thought about it."

"I want a big modern kitchen."

"What about the size? Big like Dalton's house?"

"That's too big. Maybe three quarters the size? I'd like an area large enough to host family gatherings. I know Aunt Catalina hosts everything now, but it would be nice to rotate some holidays. I think I would enjoy entertaining."

Adan's heart warmed. He could picture Lanni flawlessly

executing a holiday gathering for the growing Vargas family and the Francos.

"Thus the large kitchen?"

"Yeah. I want a huge fridge. Maybe not a chef's fridge. We could..."

We. His heart rammed against his ribcage. He wished traffic was light enough that he could steal a glimpse of her face. Unfortunately, they were stuck in a grouping of impatient drivers requiring his focus.

"I mean, I could see a second fridge in the garage. Double ovens are a must. Cook top. Microwave. Lots of storage space. A walk-in pantry."

"See, I knew you had something in mind."

"What about you? What do you want in a house?"

"Dunno. Kitchen doesn't matter too much. I'm not a cook." His eyes darted to the sleeping Jet in the back. "Guess I'll have to learn."

"Besides the kitchen, what else?"

"A theater room. I always wanted to watch sports on a gigantic screen."

"Like a theater screen?"

"Eh. Could be a huge TV. I like the idea of two rows of recliners."

Solana laughed. "So like Derin's entertainment room?"

"Yeah, only bigger."

She snorted. "Guys. Always got to one-up each other."

Adan chuckled.

As their conversation waned, he considered the owner's bedroom suite. When he pictured Solana in it, he figured he should redirect his thoughts.

"I'm not sure if I want horse property or not."

"Why not? You have horses. At least Jet's, the barrel racer, and Trixie Wind."

"Yeah, but they would probably get more exercise if I boarded them at Vargas Ranch."

"I suppose. Don't you love horses?"

"Not sure I'd want to come home after a full day of working with horses to the responsibility of exercising my own."

"I have to pee," Jet said from the back seat.

Solana tapped on her phone. "Looks like there's a rest stop in another fifteen miles. Can you make it that long?"

Jet agreed he could, so they didn't stop until they arrived at the rest stop. When Adan shut off the truck engine, he was glad for the chance to stretch his legs. They'd already been on the road for two hours. His knee complained about that.

He walked around near the truck while Jet and Solana used the facilities. Only six more hours to go. He figured they could stop in Flagstaff for longer. Maybe pick up a second breakfast or lunch—whatever places were serving when they arrived.

After they were on the road again, Adan smiled as Solana played road games with Jet.

"I spy... Something blue and orange," she said.

Jet replied, "I don't see it."

"Look out the front window."

"Oh! That truck's logo."

"Good job, Jet."

"Your turn, Adan," Jet said.

Well, he couldn't disappoint the boy. "I spy..." Adan glanced at Solana. She wore a yellow blouse with a white flower pattern. His eyes back on the road, he waited a few seconds. "Something yellow and white."

Jet scoffed. "Too easy. The stripes on the road."

"Nope."

Solana giggled but pursed her lips.

"What? There can't be anything else."

"Keep looking, bud," Adan encouraged him.

Jet craned his neck to look into the front seat, thankfully keeping his seat belt on.

"Oh, no fair. It's your girlfriend's shirt."

Adan's face felt hotter than the asphalt on an Arizona summer day.

"Good job!" Solana exclaimed.

Adan glanced over and noticed her pink cheeks. And that she didn't correct Jet's assumption. Wonder if he should read into that or not.

SOLANA'S FACE WARMED when Jet called her Adan's girl-friend. That old familiar longing tumbled in her stomach like an uneven load of laundry. How she wished it were true.

She quickly congratulated Jet on finding the something yellow and white — her blouse.

Adan went quiet and his face turned crimson. But he didn't correct Jet's assumption.

Huh. Maybe there was hope after all.

No matter how much she wanted to nurture that hope into something more, she reminded herself for the thousandth time, her role in the road trip was to help Adan and Jet. Not dream of being Adan's girlfriend or Jet's step-mom. They weren't a family. And probably never would be.

"We're almost to Flag," Adan muttered.

"It's only nine-thirty. Should we keep going until Gallup?" she asked.

"I could stand to stretch my legs." Adan rubbed his right knee. The one he had surgery on years ago. Another detail about his life she knew because of their friendship.

"If we turn onto I-40, there are a few places easily accessible from the first exit."

"Yeah," Adan replied. "I'll fill up the truck, too."

When they stopped at the gas station, Solana went inside the convenience store with Jet. She filled a large soda for herself and Adan. It wasn't unusual for them to share. She reminded Jet she had snacks in the truck, so he asked for a small soda for himself. As she paid for the drinks, she noticed Adan limping toward them.

"I would have paid."

She snorted. "You can get the next one. You know, lunch."

"Ah, the more expensive stop."

"Duh."

He laughed, and those lines near his blue eyes deepened. She loved his laugh. It was like the sun breaking through the monsoon clouds, shining a spotlight on the no longer parched desert of her heart.

Adan limped toward the truck with Solana and Jet walking beside him.

"You want me to drive?" she offered.

"Nope."

She resisted a frustrated growl. It was obvious his knee was bothering him. Instead of arguing, she handed him an ibuprofen once they settled in the truck. He grunted but accepted the medicine with a sip of the soda.

"Dr. Pepper. How did you know I was in the mood for it?"

Solana giggled. "I didn't. I was."

"Buckle up, Jet."

"Yes, sir."

Soon they were back on the highway, soft music playing in the background.

Sometimes their friendship perplexed Solana. Over the years, she and Adan had become very close. They knew everything about each other — even a few things she wished she didn't know, like his abysmal dating life. Don't get her wrong. She was glad he hadn't settled down. 'Cause as long as he didn't, she had a chance. Still, it was hard to listen to stories about the horrible women he dated. Most women started to see him as a paycheck once they learned he had been a three-time world champion pro bull rider. A few dropped him like a brick, too insecure about the perceived competition for his attention. They never got to know him like she had. Adan would be completely devoted to the woman he fell in love with.

If only that woman could be her.

Solana sighed and reached for the large soda cup. The lid popped off and soda sloshed over the sides.

"Oh, no!"

Adan fumbled with the latch to the center console while she secured the lid, sticky soda dribbling down her arm.

"Should have some napkins in here."

She set the cup back in the holder, lid firmly in place. Then she dug around in the console. Her fingers connected with a fat envelope. She pulled it out along with a wad of napkins. Then she dabbed the wet trail off her arm.

"What's this?" she asked while she blotted her shirt dry.

Adan groaned. "I forgot all about that. Can you reach my laptop bag and slide it in there?"

"Yeah."

"It's from the attorney. I think it has Jet's birth certificate and maybe some other paperwork in it. I forgot I stuffed it in there."

The muscle in Adan's jaw twitched. Solana reached over and rested her hand on his forearm.

"Hey, you've had a lot on your mind. You can read it tonight."

"Yeah."

Solana tossed the napkins into a grocery sack near her feet for trash. Then she slid the envelope into the front pocket of his laptop bag behind his seat.

"You good back there, Jet?" she asked.

"Yup. Playing a game."

"Ok. Let me know if you get hungry. I brought some of your favorites."

"Thanks."

Solana stretched her neck, wishing she could read the contents of the envelope to Adan. Her gut warned her not to in front of Jet. No telling what information the attorney put together.

When she rolled her lips inward, Adan reached over and patted her hand. "Something bugging you?"

She blew out a soft breath. "I'll be fine."

As much as she wanted to talk to him about their relationship, a road trip to his son's late mother's home wasn't the right timing. What would she say, anyway? That they acted like a couple—so much so that Jet picked up on it. That friendship and attraction could become love?

Ugh. She already loved him. She was just waiting for him to fall in love with her.

Now and then, she would catch a look in his eye that made her wonder. That fanned the tiny flame of hope. Then it would disappear, leaving her guessing if she imagined the whole thing.

Maybe this road trip would help Adan see her as a woman with motherly instincts. Maybe God would finally use it to make Adan fall in love with her.

She stopped her thoughts shy of lifting up a prayer for that. If God wanted them to become a couple, it would happen in His timing. She hoped.

5

"CAN YOU TEXT Haynes that we're almost there?" Adan asked Solana.

"On it."

He listened as the faint fake-clicking sounds came from his phone before Solana set it back in the holder. The navigation instructed them to exit the freeway and start winding through the unfamiliar streets of Albuquerque, New Mexico.

Adan's stomach churned. Could be that burger from lunch. More likely, it was stress and anxiety about what awaited him and Jet at the boy's home. His arm rested on the center console. When exactly Solana entwined her fingers with his, he hadn't noticed. He sure did like the settling affect her touch had on him. And he appreciated her support more than he could say.

He sent up prayers for Jet, knowing it would be hard for the boy to spend time in his home with strangers going through his mama's stuff.

"We're almost there," Jet said.

Adan heard the pain in his voice and his heart ached as bad as his stomach. *Lord, please.*

"This is the street."

The navigation announced their destination was on the right. Adan slowed the truck until he spotted the house number. Then he parked, checking his side mirrors to make sure the horse trailer didn't block the neighbor's driveway.

As the noise of the engine quieted, the three of them sat there in silent agreement for a minute, fully aware of the somber task ahead.

A navy blue sedan passed them on the street before parking in the driveway. Edward Haynes waved as he exited the car.

Adan unbuckled his seatbelt, quickly followed by Solana. Jet sat there staring at the house, tears trickling down his cheeks. Adan coughed at the sight.

"You okay, bud?"

Jet sniffed and rubbed the corner of his t-shirt on his face. "Yup."

Adan reached back and squeezed his knee. When Jet met his gaze, he offered a sympathetic smile.

"You got this. Remember, God is with us through it."

"Yes, sir."

"Alright, let's not keep Mr. Haynes waiting."

Solana slid down from her seat, settling her black hat on her head. She opened the door for Jet. Adan eased out, donning his tan hat. He walked stiffly for the first ten steps. Then he rounded the truck and placed a hand on Jet's shoulder, matching the boy's pace to the shaded porch.

"Mr. Franco." The attorney offered a sympathetic half-smile.

"Mr. Haynes. Thanks for meeting us." Adan shook his outstretched hand.

Edward unlocked the front door and swung it wide before handing the keys to Adan. Jet darted into the house and ducked into a bedroom, slamming the door shut.

Solana quirked an eyebrow at Adan, who sighed, scrubbing both hands down his face.

"Give him a few minutes." The words fell from his mouth, sounding far more confident than he felt. He did not know if they ought to push Jet or leave him be or something in between. How parents knew what to do was beyond him.

Edward cleared his throat. "My wife stocked the fridge

with some of Jet's favorite foods and drinks. She also put some sodas and flavored coffee creamer in there."

"Please thank her for us," Solana said. "We appreciate not having to run out to buy things right away."

The attorney handed him another envelope. "This is the paperwork on the horses. Still in Annabel's name, but I've got an appointment on the books for you on Tuesday morning to transfer ownership. That'll give you a few days before then to settle things here."

"Seems like you've thought of everything," Adan said. "Thanks."

"Please reach out if you have questions. We knew Annabel personally, too."

Adan set the envelope on the counter. Then he escorted Mr. Haynes to the door, thanking him again. After closing the door, he placed his cowboy hat on a nearby hook, running his hands through his hair and blowing out a loud breath.

Solana's soft voice floated down the hall. She must have snuck into Jet's room to comfort him.

He looked around the living space of Annabel's home. Comfy suede furniture filled the living area. A nice sized TV had been mounted to the wall. He'd have to figure out how to take that down. Rustic wood end tables sat on both sides of the couch and one next to an overstuffed chair. A romance book rested on it. Annabel's.

Reality nearly doubled him over. Annabel was gone in an instant at such a young age. She left behind a hurting son, two horses, and all this.

The walls closed in, so Adan burst out of the house into the bright afternoon sun. He bent over, rubbing his hands on his thighs for several seconds before straightening. This was gonna be even harder than he expected. How could Annabel be gone?

Shaking off the thought, he retrieved their luggage from the truck bed. Then he set them inside the house. Solana sat on the overstuffed chair, flipping through the pages of the book he noticed earlier.

"He okay?"

She shrugged. "He's missing his mama."

Adan expelled a loud breath.

"You mind watching him for a bit? There's still enough daylight for me to head over to the ranch that's boarding the horses. I want to see if they'd mind me dropping off the trailer. Don't think the neighbors want the eyesore sitting on their nice subdivision street for a week."

"Of course. You might let him know you're leaving."

"Yeah. Good idea."

Adan ambled down the hall. Pictures of Jet and Annabel lined the wall. From his birth all the way to his latest school picture. Adan reached up and brushed his fingers over the most recent picture of Annabel. As he remembered fragmented moments from their rodeo days, his feelings toward her seemed brotherly, not romantic.

What an awesome, frightening, and heavy responsibility she entrusted to him. Adan swallowed down the lump in his throat as he eased Jet's bedroom door open.

"Jet."

The boy sprawled on his stomach, head buried in his pillow. His cowboy boots laid askew on the floor as if he had kicked them off as an afterthought. At the sound of his name, he slowly rolled over and sat upright.

"I'm gonna drop the trailer off at the ranch. Solana is staying here. Let her know if you need anything."

"Adan?"

"Yeah, bud?"

"Can I... Hug?"

Adan blinked back the stinging in his eyes as he opened his arms wide. Jet pushed off the bed and fell against him, gripping his waist for a solid minute. Maybe two. Adan rubbed a hand over Jet's back. His son.

Lord, I sure hope You know what You're doing here. 'Cause

this is breaking my heart in two.

SOLANA SNUCK DOWN the hall, wiping the moisture from her eyes as she prayed fervently for Adan and Jet. He was turning out to be a natural father. Confident. Comforting. Gentle.

Shouldn't surprise her. He had an amazing example in Harley Franco. And years of watching Uncle Tres and her dad, too. Lots of godly men to emulate.

Besides, Adan trusted God wholeheartedly. Whatever he didn't know how to navigate, she knew God would lead him.

She straightened her back and grabbed her suitcase. Wheeling it down the hall, she passed Jet's room on the right and a bathroom on the left before stopping at the second bedroom on the right. She would leave the owner's room for Adan.

The guest room contained a full size bed nestled between two windows. Frilly curtains dressed up the windows with a view into the small backyard. A dresser sat along one wall and a small desk on the other. White single panel sliding doors hid the closet's contents.

Solana opened the closet doors, relieved to find a few hangers. She gently set her suitcase on the neutral beige comforter. Then she unpacked her things, hanging up her shirts and dresses. She opened each of the dresser drawers, thankful they were empty. The last of her things filled two of the four dresser drawers.

"Miss Solana."

"Back here."

She tucked her empty suitcase in the closet and met Jet in the hallway.

"Can I have a snack?"

"Sure. Let's see what we've got."

She led the way to the quaint kitchen, complete with a small island flanked by three bar stools. Jet flumped onto one of them. She opened the stainless steel fridge. A bulk-sized package of string cheese begged to be eaten.

"String cheese?"

"Yeah. I'll take two."

Solana opened the package and grabbed three, handing two to Jet. She leaned back against the counter.

"I'm guessing you like string cheese and Mrs. Haynes knows it?"

"Yup."

Jet pulled apart the ends of the plastic surrounding the first one. Then he bit off a huge chunk of the cheese.

Solana laughed. "No, no, no. You can't eat it like that!"

She opened her own piece and coaxed a few strands of the cheese from the rest. Then she tilted her head back and let it curl onto her tongue.

"That's how you eat string cheese."

Jet smiled, though it didn't quite reach his eyes. "No. That's how *you* eat string cheese. This is how *I* do it."

He bit off another huge chunk and chewed it with exaggerated mouth smacking.

She smiled. "Guess we'll have to agree to disagree on that one."

Solana offered him a soda, knowing she probably shouldn't allow him too much of the sugary beverage. She would pay more attention tomorrow. Today, he needed grace and kindness more than correction.

"Looks like Mrs. Haynes left a meal. Says it's a mexicali casserole."

"It's good. She brought them by lots when Mama..."

Solana heard his unspoken words: when Mama was sick, but still at home.

"Miss Solana? Can I ask you something?"

"Sure."

"How well do you know Adan? Is he a... is he good?"

"Oh, sweetie. He's the best of men. A loyal friend. Godly. He prays for so many people and everyone knows they can count on him."

Though now he would need to rely on his friends, including her, through this tough transition.

Jet slumped and his eyes flicked away. A frown flashed across his face. "Why didn't he come visit me?"

Solana swallowed a sip of her soda before answering. "Your mom never told him about you. If she had, he would have been here a long time ago."

"How do you know?"

"Because Adan is my best friend. I know how much he cares about other people. If he had known he had a son? Well, stampeding cattle couldn't keep him away."

A throat cleared from the other end of the room. Solana's eyes snapped to Adan's. He stood in front of the closed door, making her wonder just how much of their conversation he had heard.

After toeing off his boots and placing his hat on a hook, he joined her in the kitchen. He dropped the bags of road snacks on the counter. Then he eased his laptop bag from his shoulder onto a nearby stool, stuffing the envelope with the paperwork for the horses in the front pocket.

"She's right, you know," he said. "If I had known about you, I would have come right away. Done anything to be a part of your life."

Jet chugged the rest of his soda and stared at the hallway. Solana knew it would take time before Jet trusted Adan enough to believe it.

"You want to hang out in your room?" Adan asked.

"Yeah."

"Go ahead. Solana and I will figure out dinner and let you know when it's ready."

Jet scuffed down the hall.

Adan winked at her. "Best friend, huh?"

Solana smiled as she retrieved the mexicali casserole from the fridge. She bumped him away from the stove with her hip.

"You know you are."

Ugh. The dreamy quality of her voice gave away too many of her feelings.

"Lanni."

His husky tone sent pleasant tingles down her spine. She punched the buttons on the stove to preheat it before she turned toward him. He reached for her hands and held them tight.

"Thank you."

Heat warmed her cheeks. "Of course."

Adan shook her hands up and down to emphasize his words. "I'm serious. Thank you for this. I had no idea how badly I needed you with me. Not just anyone. You. My best friend."

She swallowed away the sudden dryness in her throat as she studied his deep blue eyes. She loved him so much. Would do anything for him.

Solana glanced at the stove as she extracted her hands from his. She needed a little space, or she might tell him she loved him. Humor always helped her to deflect her true feelings.

"So I've dethroned Dylan as your bestie?"

Adan laughed. "Yeah, I think so. I haven't updated him yet about Jet."

She preened, surprised by his revelation. Maybe there was more hope for a relationship with Adan than she thought.

"Let me put this in the oven and I can help you with the owner's suite. I'm guessing all her clothes are here. We can put them in trash bags and find a donation center."

Adan coughed. "Thanks. That'd be great."

She heard him wheel his suitcase down the hall as she slid the casserole into the hot oven. She set a timer on her phone before sliding it into her jeans pocket. Then she grabbed several trash bags from under the kitchen sink and headed down the hall to the owner's room.

Adan set his laptop bag on the desk under the large window with a view of the backyard. A queen bed stood centered along one side of the room. The closet and owner's bath entrance was on the opposite side.

Solana tossed the trash bags on the bathroom vanity. Then she entered the closet. As she suspected, it was full of Annabel Garrison's clothing. Shaking out a trash bag, Solana filled it with shoes. Then she folded dresses and stacked them neatly in a second bag.

By the time she filled four bags, the timer sounded for the casserole. She punched it off and entered the bedroom. Adan sat on the corner of the bed, staring at the dresser.

"I can't bring myself to open it. It seems... I don't know. Wrong?"

She crossed the room and rubbed her hand on his back, wishing she could ease his burden.

"Like I'm invading her privacy."

"I'll empty them out after supper."

His shoulders relaxed, and he expelled a loud breath. "Thanks."

"Would you mind taking what I've bagged up and put it in the garage? I was thinking of sticking a sheet of paper on the garage walls. One for donations, which these are. One for trash. And one to move."

Adan quirked a grin. "Huh. You *are* the smart one, after all."

She play-shoved his arm before pivoting toward the kitchen, smiling the entire way. She donned the oven mitts and removed the casserole from the oven. Then she searched through cupboards and drawers to find three place settings for the table.

"Jet! Adan! Supper is ready!"

Jet scuffed into the room. "I'm starving!"

Adan chuckled. "Me too."

"Jet, can you get us drinks?" she asked. "I'll take an ice water."

He placed their drinks on the table as she carried the casserole over to it. The spicy aroma filled the air, making her mouth water. Guess she was hungry, too. She balanced a serving spatula on the dish and took her seat.

After Adan prayed, she dished up the meal. She kept the conversation light, sensing Adan's troubled mood and empathizing with Jet's grief. When they finished, Jet took off for his room again.

"I'll get the dishes," Adan said.

"Alright. I'll work on the dresser in your room."

Solana grabbed a few more trash bags from under the sink.

"I'll see about picking up moving boxes tomorrow."

"Sounds good," she replied before hurrying down the hall.

Out of the three of them, she figured she would be the least affected by going through Annabel's things. She was a stranger. Still, it felt weird and a little disturbing to bag up all Jet's mom's clothes, underwear, shoes, and toiletries. She could only imagine what was running through Adan's mind.

6

———

ADAN BRACED HIS palms on the counter as Solana walked away. He felt like he was watching someone else's life on a movie screen. Sitting down to eat at the table Annabel picked out. Washing her dishes. Caring for her son.

His stomach sank as the image of her things in the dresser seared into his brain. Her unmentionables. Things he shouldn't see or know what they looked like. It seemed very wrong.

And that confused him, too. If he had made love to her thirteen years ago, it shouldn't bother him, right?

No matter how many memories flitted in and out of his thoughts, Adan couldn't recall one romantic feeling, touch, or act with Annabel Garrison. She had been like a sister to him. Good friends. Never anything more.

But, Jet…

Adan growled and pushed away from the counter. He stacked the dishes and loaded the dishwasher. Then he dropped a pod into the dispenser and started it. Thank goodness for Mrs. Haynes' foresight to make sure they had things like that on hand.

Solana rounded the corner with two more full trash bags.

"There's three more back there for donation."

He headed that way as she entered the garage. The door slammed shut behind her with a rattling *thud*. He snagged the three bags and passed Solana as she headed back to the owner's suite. How much more was there to sort through tonight?

Shoving the garage door open with his foot, he stepped over the threshold. The garage held a few bins stacked neatly in a corner next to a small work table. He had not expected to see a car in the garage—a mid-size silver sedan. Older but still in decent shape.

Adan tossed the bags into the donation pile and examined the car more closely. He opened the door. Odometer showed over one hundred thirty thousand miles on the Honda. The interior appeared clean, with some signs of its age. Tire tread looked good. Guess he'd have to figure out what to do with it. Donate? Sell?

Walking through the laundry room, he sighed. Again. Seemed to be doing a heap of that. *Lord, I could use your wisdom for the dozens of decisions before me. Help me see a clear path.*

When he passed Jet's room, he backtracked and knocked on the door.

"Jet?"

A grunt sounded before the door opened.

"Can I come in?"

The dark-haired kid swung the door wide and flopped onto his bed.

Adan studied him for a second. Red around his eyes. Dark circles underneath. Mouth pulled into a tight line.

He eased onto the corner of Jet's bed as his chest tightened.

"Just wanted to talk about the plan for the next while."

A cloud shadowed the boy's eyes.

"I'll need you go through your things to decide what to pack for the move and what to donate."

A few silent seconds ticked by to the sound of Jet's laptop fan running hard. Hmm. Wasn't sure he was fond of the kid having a computer in his room. He'd have to do some research about if that was a good idea or not.

"Think about what you'll need right away until we get a house. Whatever you can do without for a few months, then we'll box it up. If you have things you want to get rid of, we'll decide if it's trash or can be donated."

Jet cleared his throat. "What about my mama's stuff?"

Adan reached out and squeezed his shoulder. "Solana has gone through the clothes and toiletries. Anything of value, you can say if you want to keep it or not. We'll probably keep most of the furniture, unless you think it's too painful to see it all the time. We may want it for the house."

Jet snorted. "What house?"

"The one we're gonna move into in Arizona. Once we find it."

"Fine. Do I have to start tonight?"

"Nope. If you want to hang out or watch TV until bedtime, that's fine."

After Jet's curt nod, Adan stood and headed to the owner's suite.

Solana looked up from her perch on the edge of the bed. Her compassionate smile and bright eyes warmed him from head to toe.

"That's all the clothes and consumables. You'll need to go through her desk. And Jet and I will go through her jewelry and rodeo awards sometime this week."

Adan crossed the room and pulled her into his arms, burying his face against her neck. She rubbed her hands up and down his back, giving no sign of wanting to break the connection. He breathed deeply of her fruity scent. Maybe her bodywash or shampoo. He couldn't quite place the fragrance, nor did he have the brainpower to think about it. After several minutes, he released her.

"Don't." She held up a finger. "You've thanked me plenty already. Let's agree that I accept your gratitude and you don't have to keep saying it. Deal?"

He slid his hands down her arms. She hummed softly as goosebumps appeared behind the trail of his fingers. The more he considered her reaction, he realized she felt the same zing of attraction for him as he did for her. If he wasn't so exhausted, he would jump for joy.

"Deal."

"I'm gonna decompress before calling it a night."

"Alright. See you in the morning, Lanni."

After she left, Adan unpacked his things in the now empty dresser, closet, and bathroom. Then he retrieved his laptop and the envelopes from the attorney. Setting them on the bed, he propped all the pillows on one side before easing against them and the headboard.

He donned his reading glasses. Then he ran a finger along the flap of the envelope Haynes gave him the day he brought Jet to Arizona. Flipping through several pages, he noticed Jet's birth certificate, information about Jet's school in Albuquerque, his social security card, and more.

Sure enough, there in black and white on the birth certificate was the father: Adan Samuel Franco with his birth date and city included.

He carefully returned Jet's paperwork to the envelope. When his fingers connected with a smaller sealed envelope inside, he pulled it out. Shaky letters spelled out his name.

Adan's pulse spiked and sweat beaded on his forehead. He swiped it away, rubbing his hand on his jeans. Then he shot to his feet. He needed a minute before reading it.

He walked down the hall to Jet's room to pray with his son before warning him lights out in fifteen minutes. Then he returned to Annabel's room.

After changing into a loose t-shirt and gym shorts, he reclined on the bed, donned the readers, and opened the envelope. Several double-sided pages contained what he now recognized as Annabel's handwriting, though shakier than the documents on her desk.

He prepared himself as best he could for what she would reveal beyond the grave.

Adan,

By now, I'm sure you are confused about the mess I've left you to deal with. I'm sorry. When Jet was born over twelve years ago, I never imagined the waves one small decision would cause in his life or yours. Oh! Or your wife's. Please, let her read this too, as I'm sure you must have married long ago.

Let me start at the beginning.

Adan continued to read Annabel's full confession. How Jet had been conceived. Her struggles after leaving the rodeo. Her gratitude for Adan's role in leading her to a relationship with Jesus. All a baffling tale.

He sat upright, hanging his legs over the edge of the bed. He worked his hands over his thighs trying to make sense of what she said. She answered many of his questions but spawned dozens more.

Adan launched to his feet. He needed to talk to someone. Work through this now.

As he eased his door open, he cringed. Solana's light was off and soft snores sounded from within. He really ought to let her sleep, but he was far too desperate to act rationally.

The hinges squealed as he swung the door open. No going back now.

"LANNI. LANNI!"

A harsh whisper and a hearty shake of her shoulders jolted her from a sweet dream which slipped from her mind before she could savor it. Drat.

"Lanni."

"Adan?"

She groaned and rolled over.

"What time is it?"

"Late. I need to talk to you. Annabel left me a letter."

Solana's heart jump-started and she sat upright. Adan clasped her hand and tugged, pulling her from the guest room and into his.

"Sit."

He pointed to the bed, and her insides twisted in knots with a sickening feeling. This seemed like a bad idea. The room filled with a restless energy as his frenzied pacing left subtle footprints in the thick carpet.

"Adan," she whined. "Can't this wait until morning?"

He planted his feet, pivoting suddenly toward her. As their eyes locked, she could see the wildness within his gaze, like a storm raging in the depths of his soul.

"No. Read it. It's right there."

Solana sighed, wiping the sleep from her eyes. She reached for the chicken scratch and scanned the letter.

Huh. Annabel assumed Adan had married. Probably a reasonable thought, given his charm and — She should finish reading.

Jet is not your son.

The words socked her hard in the gut. She read them aloud as if that would help them make more sense. "Jet is not your son?"

"Keep reading."

Adan stopped his frantic pacing and settled onto the bed, back against the stack of pillows.

"No child should ever learn that he had been conceived through... Jet's biological father forced himself on..."

Solana let her hand fall to her lap, letter and all.

"Is she serious, Adan? You aren't the father. His real father... He..."

"Yes."

A sob strangled Solana's words as she imagined enduring that. And deciding to carry the child. Give birth. And raise him. Everyday seeing a miniature of a horrible...

Adan pulled her to him as she cried. She respected Annabel tenfold for all the tough choices she had made for Jet's benefit.

Solana rested her head against Adan's chest. "I can't bear to read more."

"She was afraid his father would find out and try to take Jet away. Or worse, raise him if anything happened to her."

"So she put your name on the birth certificate?"

"Yeah."

She looked up at Adan now. The deep creases in his forehead aged him beyond his thirty-five years.

"Annabel had never been close to her family. She said she picked me because of my character and our friendship. She knew I would be a good father." Adan shook his head. "How could she know that? I don't believe it myself."

Solana flattened her hand against his chest and held his gaze. "Because she knew you like I do. You are a godly man. Even when you were twenty-two and making a few less-than-Christian choices, I'm sure who you are in here —" She patted his heart. "You were still a good man."

"Lanni..."

"Is there more?"

"The short version is that she never thought I would know. That she'd raise Jet to adulthood. But just in case, she wanted to ensure it would be easy for me to assume guardianship. As his father on his birth certificate, there would be no obstacles."

His gaze darted to the corner of the room. "Unless..."

"Unless you forced a paternity test."

"Exactly. And I thought about it when Haynes first brought Jet."

"But you won't?"

He shook his head. "Especially not now, knowing..."

"Did she say who the father was?"

"No. She said she was the only one who knew. He would never admit what he did to her. And she wanted to take the knowledge to her grave, believing it was best for Jet."

Solana scooted upright, patting the moisture from her cheeks. She studied Adan for several minutes.

"Is there more?"

"She asked me to burn her confession after my wife read it. So, do I keep it until I get married and risk Jet accidentally discovering it?"

"Look, she asked you to burn it after your wife read it because she assumed you were married. She made it clear Jet could never know, right?"

"Right."

"And since you're going to be his father, if you marry—" The words knifed her heart. "Your future wife will know you are a single dad. She never needs to know the full story."

"I don't know."

Solana shook her head. "Adan, we must burn it. Tonight."

Then she bounced to the edge of the bed and sprang off. She took his hand and the letter, leading him into the owner's bathroom.

"Got a lighter?"

"We aren't burning it now. What if we burn down the house?"

She opened and closed a few drawers until she found the candle lighter she had seen earlier and figured they could pack it and the scented candles in the move.

"We won't burn the house down." She pointed to the ceiling. "No smoke detector in the bathroom. Sink is marble. We tear it up and burn small pieces in the sink."

She handed the letter to him. When he did nothing, she took the first sheet and tore it into quarters. Then she lit one on fire and dropped it into the sink basin. When it turned to ash, she continued with the next piece. While she burned pieces, Adan ripped the remaining pages, handing them to her in small batches. Once the last remnant turned to ash, Solana ran water down the drain and wiped out the sink.

"There. You and I are the only two people who know the truth."

Adan closed his eyes, letting his hands drop to his side.

"You know you can trust me," she said.

"With my life. And that of my son's."

"Good."

Then he pulled her into his arms and clutched her tightly, as if he needed to borrow some of her strength. Solana relaxed in his hold as her hands tenderly caressed his back. As he leaned slightly away, his eyes locked on hers before his gaze darted to her lips. His hand lodged deep in her thick hair right before she leaned into his warmth, tilting her face upwards as she closed her eyes.

When his lips moved over hers tentatively at first, she responded. Adan's hands roamed over her back, and he fervently pressed closer, sending waves of delight over her. Then the kiss ended as tenderly as it had begun, exceeding all her dreams of a first kiss with him.

A husky hum rose in his throat.

"I probably shouldn't have kissed you."

Despite his words, he maintained his hold.

"Do you see me running away?" she teased.

"Maybe you should."

When their arms untangled, the physical space between them grew wider.

"Good night, Lanni."

He motioned for her to leave his room. Ah, well. Maybe this time he was the smart one.

As Solana darted across the hall into the darkness of her room, she smiled. Adan Franco kissed her. At last!

7

THE NEXT MORNING, Adan woke to the smell of bacon. His mouth watered as he groaned, slinging his long legs over the side of the strange bed. Annabel's bed.

Yeah, he would donate it instead of moving it. Too weird to think of using it. The bed in the guest room would work until he bought something for himself.

As he padded toward the kitchen, a groggy Jet joined him in the hall.

"Sleep okay?"

A grunt came from the preteen as his movements reminded Adan of the sloth character in his nephew's favorite movie. Whatever speed was less than slow — that's how Jet trudged.

When Adan entered the kitchen, the sight of Solana cooking in her pjs caused his heart to ram against his rib cage worse than those old bulls he rode. She looked… Perfectly homey and sexy and everything he wanted in a wife with her long dark waves piled on the top of her head in a sloppy bun. Her silky neck peeked out from the top of her fitted sleep shirt. Those wide-legged pajama pants made her waist look slim and her hips curvy. He snorted when he noticed the vintage cowgirl pattern. Fun pjs that fit his Lanni's personality.

"Smells good," he said.

Solana whirled around and Adan chuckled at the words

emblazoned on the sleep shirt. *Cowgirls are too smarter.*

She waved a hand in front of it. "Told you I was the smart one."

"How can I help?"

"Set the table?"

"Done."

Jet finally arrived in the kitchen and oozed onto a chair like a spineless blob of goo. Mornings were gonna be interesting.

"Jet, you want bacon, eggs, and toast?" Solana asked. "Mrs. Haynes bought a box of cereal that I'm guessing you like."

Something that sounded kinda like the word "cereal" came from his son's mouth. So Adan grabbed a bowl, the cereal, and milk. Then he placed them in front of Jet.

"Sorry, no biscuits," Solana said as she carried a heaping bowl of scrambled eggs and a plate of bacon to the table. The toaster popped up four slices of bread. Nice. He'd pack the big toaster for sure. She tossed them on another plate and brought it to the table.

Once she scooted in her chair, Adan prayed before piling his plate full. He ate a bite of the eggs, which were even fluffier than what they served in the dining hall.

"This is delicious. Better'n Chef's."

As pink splotched her cheeks, Adan held back a grin. He loved when Solana acted all embarrassed over a genuine compliment.

"Where'd you learn to make the eggs so fluffy?"

"My mom. She had me and Rennie helping in the kitchen early on. And, of course, with family dinner at Aunt Catalina's house, I had to become an accomplished cook."

Jet hunched over his bowl of cereal, rapidly shoveling it into his mouth, teeth crunching it loudly. Then he reached for some bacon.

"I figured we could get out around eleven. Go pick up some moving boxes and stop for lunch on the way back."

Solana looked up from the meal, her face brightening. "That sounds like a great way to break up the day."

Jet flashed a glare before staring at his empty cereal bowl. Adan swallowed down a response. He must allow the boy a chance to grieve.

"I was thinking… Tomorrow is Saturday, and the forecast is for sunshine and mild temperatures. Maybe we could go over to the Lazy D and see Optimus."

Jet's gold eyes snapped to his, a jolt of surprise written in them, instantly calming Adan's doubts. His son needed a reason to smile, something familiar and fun to lift his spirits. What better than time with his beloved horse. Maybe Adan could do this fatherhood thing after all.

"Can we?"

"Yup. I spoke with the owners and they said Silver Streak might enjoy a ride." Adan turned his attention to Solana. "And they could find a horse for me. They have miles of trails we can explore."

"I love that idea."

Her soft smile warmed his heart as he finished munching on the buttered toast. He sent up a prayer of gratitude for thinking of it. Until Solana said it aloud, Adan hadn't realized how important it would be to take breaks during their time in Albuquerque. Get out of the house and do something fun.

"Jet, what church did you attend?"

He shrugged. "Something community church. About fifteen minutes away."

Solana asked, "Did Mrs. Haynes go there too?"

"Yeah."

She shifted to look at Adan. "I'll text her this afternoon for service times and directions."

"Thanks—"

At Solana's raised eyebrow, he pursed his lips shut. She had warned him last night to stop thanking her. Only it was hard. Every simple act of service she did felt like a huge blessing to him. Her cooking breakfast. Tackling Annabel's clothes. Texting the attorney's wife. Probably seemed insignificant to her. Not to him, though. He appreciated it all.

Jet pushed back from the table, wooden chair legs scraping against the tile.

"You all done, Jet?" Solana asked.

"Yeah."

"Can you load your dirty dishes in the dishwasher? I'll get the rest while you shower."

A grunt and compliance was his response. Adan scrubbed a hand over his beard, wondering if all kids his age communicated like that. He couldn't remember being that way, but it had been a long time since he'd been a kid.

When Solana started clearing the dishes, Adan stood and helped her. The silverware clinked against the plates as he stacked them.

"I'll get this," he said.

She waved her hand in the air, not making eye contact. "You go get ready for the day. I need something to do while Jet finishes. Shared bathroom and all."

The uncomfortable silence stretched while she placed the leftovers in the fridge. When she turned around and still wouldn't make eye contact, he remembered their kiss in the middle of the night. The one he had envisioned for years. Reality had been so much better. The feel of her in his arms. The softness of her lips pressed against his. Had he only imagined she returned his kiss? Maybe it bothered her.

Clearing his throat, he dipped his head and rubbed a hand over the back of his neck. "About last night."

Finally, her dark eyes connected with his. Pink spread across her cheeks as she held his gaze, unwavering, while drumming her fingernails on the quartz countertop.

Adan looked away first, running a hand through his hair. "I... You... Me..."

"Are you going to apologize for it?" she asked, her words a mere whisper, but the frustration in her eyes spoke volumes.

Did she want him to? Or would she be mad if he did? "No. I… It wasn't the best timing."

Solana stepped into his space—close enough he could pull her into an embrace, yet far enough that they didn't have to touch at all. He studied her makeup-free face. A few faint freckles dotted her skin in random places. Her lashes looked less pronounced, though still framed her dark eyes splendidly. This was a different Solana than he had seen before. So beautiful and real.

"Adan." She whispered his name breathlessly before she straightened her shoulders. "Tell me. Did it mean anything?"

It meant everything to him, no matter how horribly timed. Late last night, his walls had dropped, exposing his heart. He let her in and she handled it with tender care. The kiss, though impulsive, reflected his true feelings for her.

Her hopeful expression dimmed as she turned away, shoulders collapsing forward.

"It didn't."

"Lanni." He clasped her upper arm, spinning her around to face him. Then he rested his hand on her soft cheek. "It meant a lot." He traced the smooth skin over her cheekbone, as her fingers curled lightly against his wrist. Her eyes glistened before a frown stamped it out.

"Don't. If you don't have feelings for me… I can't. Adan, my heart can't take the doubt."

Then a thousand interactions with her danced across his vision. Her special smile for him when he popped by the resort office, hoping to steal a few moments with her. Her eagerness to help him, no matter what. The way she teased him—flirted with him. It all added up to more than friendship. She told him as much in the way she had returned his kiss last night.

Solana Vargas cared for him.

Adan dropped his hand to his side, despite wanting—no

craving—to pull her into his arms. The timing was wrong, wrong, wrong. Jet should be his priority. He had more than enough on his plate without adding romance and wishful thinking to it.

"It meant a lot, Lanni, but now isn't the time. I need. More time. I'm sor—"

"Don't you dare apologize, Adan Franco, for the best kiss of my life."

As her tears brimmed and spilled down her cheeks, she attacked the loading of the dishwasher, ending the conversation. Adan backed away, heart simultaneously hopeful and despairing.

Then the corner of his mouth inched higher as he headed to the owner's suite. Solana Vargas had called his kiss the best of her life.

GREAT. JUST GREAT.

Solana forcefully deposited each plate into the lower section of the dishwasher. The tinking of the silverware sounded loud in the still house as she dropped them one by one into the holder. The bowls, glasses, and pans made a similar racket as she took out her embarrassment on them.

She might as well have plastered a sign on her forehead saying: *Hopelessly in love with you.*

And what did Adan mean? *It meant a lot.* A lot how? Did he have feelings for her? Had she read his kiss correctly?

Wrong timing. Yeah, he had that right. Worst timing in the world. Right after he became a single dad and while they were in his son's mother's house packing it up. *Good one, Solana. Way to go with that disastrous timing.*

Except...

She hadn't started the kiss. Adan had.

Huh.

As Solana started the dishwasher, she allowed herself to ponder the thought. Adan Franco had started the kiss. Not her.

And it meant a lot to him.

Perhaps all hope wasn't lost if she could learn to be more patient. Give him a chance to adapt to fatherhood. Buy a house. Settle into his new life. Then maybe they could talk about them. Their feelings for each other.

Solana finished wiping down the stove, counter, and table. Then she padded over to the bookshelf lining one wall of the great room. Covered in knickknacks, photos, and romance books. She would ask Adan if he minded her keeping some books she hadn't read yet. The rest they could donate, as she doubted he or Jet would want to keep them.

While she flipped through the titles, creating two stacks, she replayed their kiss and the awkward conversation. Yeah, there was truly something to build on. Feelings on both sides.

"All done!" Jet shouted down the hall before escaping to his room. The door snicked shut behind him.

After she picked an outfit for the day, she entered the bathroom. Then she showered and applied makeup. As she dropped her things in the guest room, Jet's heated words filtered down the hall.

"Why can't we live here?"

"I told you. My job is in Wickenburg."

"But this is our house. My friends are here. Why can't you get a new job here?"

When Solana approached the great room, she caught Adan's exasperated sigh. He ran a hand through his hair, evidence of his growing frustration. She silently prayed for him.

"My family, friends, and job are in Arizona."

Jet scowled and crossed his arms over his chest. "So your friends are more important than mine?"

"That's not what I mean."

Jet growled and scurried to his room, slamming the door so hard the pictures in the hallway vibrated.

"How do you explain a job to a twelve-year-old?"

When Adan's shoulders slumped, Solana stepped closer. "Sounded like you did."

"Lanni, I don't know how to do this. He has a point. What makes my friends and family more important than his?"

"He's just working through his feelings. Probably grew up in this house. He lost his mom. Of course, he wants to stay where some part of his life is familiar."

She reached out and touched Adan's forearm until he looked at her. His damp hair and blue eyes set butterflies loose in her stomach. She ignored the feeling, pressing on.

"You're the adult. So you decide what's best for both of you. And even if moving here sounds like it could work, you'll need family and friends to support you."

Guilt gnawed at her stomach as she acknowledged her selfish motives for desperately wanting Adan to stay in Arizona.

"Do you want to leave Vargas Ranch?"

Adan's eyes darted to the corner of the room. "No."

"Then it's settled."

When he blew out a long breath, she tugged on his hand.

"Let's get out of here for a few hours. Go pick up the boxes. It will be good for him."

"Alright. Let me go get him."

A few minutes later, Solana sat comfortably in the passenger seat of Adan's truck, and found directions to a store where they could buy moving boxes. Flipping down the visor, she peered into the mirror, silently praying that Jet would eventually come to accept the changes that had been thrust upon him.

With the navigation on her phone guiding their way, she turned on the satellite radio, hoping that the soothing music would help alleviate the conflict between Adan and Jet.

Once at the store, Solana watched both Adan and Jet closely. Jet narrowed his eyes each time Adan glanced at him. She sighed.

"Hey, Jet. Can you grab the red tape gun behind you?" Adan asked. "And a pack of tape?"

Jet unfolded his arms and did as Adan asked before sliding the items across the checkout counter.

Solana snagged a stack of standard sized moving boxes before joining them at the checkout. After Adan paid for the items, Jet slouched in the back seat while she helped Adan load the boxes into the truck bed.

"There's a park nearby," she mentioned to Adan. "What do you think about walking around for a bit?"

"Yeah. It's a nice day."

Within minutes, they arrived at the park. Adan held the door for her as she slid down from the high passenger seat. As they strolled through the park, the warmth of the midday sun on her back seemed to intensify the feeling of contentment that washed over her. Adan's hand clasped firmly in hers created an invisible shield that made her feel safe and needed. She could feel her heartbeat syncing with his, a rhythmic reassurance that she belonged next to him.

The scent of Adan's musky body wash lingered in the surrounding air. The familiar scent awakened memories of shared moments and deepened her connection with him. Solana thought he sensed it, too.

"I wish I could help him feel better about all this," Adan said as he twined his fingers with hers.

She savored the warmth of his long, calloused fingers. Things like that felt both natural and foreign. It was something couples did, not good, platonic friends. Thoughts of their late night kiss brought heat to her face. She forced herself to concentrate on the topic at hand and offered advice.

"Time and prayer are the two things that help grief the most."

Adan angled his head toward her. "When did you become so wise?"

She shrugged. "Guess I listen to Mom and Aunt Catalina more than I realized."

He chuckled. When Jet shot a look over his shoulder, Adan sobered and lowered his voice. "I am praying for him. I used to think I understood what the Bible meant by praying continuously. Over these last few days, I feel like I'm praying more than ever."

Solana leaned against his arm. "Me too. I'm praying for you both. And how I can best help you."

"Thanks, Lanni."

"Hey, I thought we agreed you don't have to keep doing that."

He winked at her. "I'm the pretty one, remember?"

She snorted. "I think you might have hit your head one too many times riding those bulls."

"Good thing you're the smart one."

"Speaking of smart… What do you say we grab some lunch?"

"Let's do it."

With a warm smile on her face, she watched as he let go of her hand and swiftly jogged towards Jet. The chilly air nipped at her skin, causing her to tuck her freezing hands deep into the cozy pockets of her jacket. A longing sensation washed over her as she yearned for Adan's comforting touch. Perhaps this trip would be the catalyst to shatter the remaining walls that stood between them.

8

THE NEXT DAY, Adan winced at the screeching packing tape as he sealed the last box of books Solana wanted to keep. Then he set the tape gun on the kitchen counter before flicking his wrist to read the time.

"I think that's good for now. What do you say we head on over to the Lazy D?"

For the first time since Adan met Jet, the boy's eyes sparkled with pure delight. He ran to his room and returned a few seconds later, nearly tripping as he tried to stuff his feet into his boots while running down the hall.

Adan laughed. "Slow down, bud."

Solana giggled. "I'm sure we won't leave without you."

While she packed some snacks and beverages into a grocery sack, Adan donned his boots, hat, and denim jacket. Then he helped Solana into hers. She adjusted her hat and waited for him to unlock the house. The moment he opened the door, Jet ran to the truck.

"Come on. You're so slow!"

Adan chuckled as he wrapped his free hand around Solana's. He liked the feel of her smaller hand in his. When he glanced at her, his pace slowed. It'd be so easy to lower his head and allow his lips to brush across hers. The idea seemed perfectly normal—like they belonged together. Something deep inside of him loosened at the thought.

She flashed him a mischievous grin before she sprinted

away from him. "Race ya!"

His heart bucked like those crazy old bulls. He loved the way she egged him on. Hurrying to catch up, he reached for the truck door handle. Right as her fingers curled through it, so did his.

"Allow me."

That sweet, shy embarrassment turned her cheeks pink. Her dark eyes hid behind her sweeping lashes. Adan held the door open for her and waited until she buckled in before closing the door. Then he dropped the bag of snacks in the back and climbed behind the wheel.

Solana's fragrance teased his senses on the drive to the ranch, nearly drowning out Jet's excited chatter about his horse. Adan focused on the road, only half-listening to Solana's questions and Jet's answers.

The three of them together headed for an afternoon outing; they felt like a family. Maybe that's why he'd been reaching for Lanni's hand more and more lately. Or why he kissed her two nights ago.

He slowed the truck as he turned off the main road. A rustic metal sign spanned the entrance to the Lazy D Ranch. A sprawling stucco home stood at the end of the lane, which veered left toward a large pasture and stables. Adan drove slowly as his tires crunched over the thick gravel. In the distance, a mountain broke against the bright blue sky, reminding him of the scenic views back home.

"There he is!" Jet exclaimed. "That's Optimus grazing."

Then Adan recognized Annabel's barrel racer, Silver Streak. His mood plummeted as a dozen rodeos flashed across his memory. Annabel's serious scowl as she concentrated on her patterns. Silver Streak's amazing speed. The high fives she exchanged with him. The light in Annabel's eyes when she won—much like the joy in Jet's gold eyes now.

Adan coughed to mask the grief the images evoked. They had been good friends. Never more. Yet she trusted him to raise her son. He still couldn't believe she was gone.

And that was only a small glimpse of what Jet had to feel. Annabel was his mama. The one who raised him. Comforted him in sorrow. Praised his achievements. Fixed his scrapes and bruises.

Adan felt so inadequate for the job of father.

As soon as he cut the truck engine, Jet raced out to the fence line, calling for his horse. The black gelding's mane blew in the wind as he trotted toward Jet. When the boy ran his hand over his horse's face, Adan swallowed the lump in his throat at the sight of their deep connection. Perhaps prayer, time, and his horse might lessen the sting of grief.

"Adan!" Cooper Dunbar greeted him as his very pregnant wife lumbered toward them, resting her hand under her baby bump. "This is my wife, Emeline."

Adan shook his hand first, then hers, before introducing Solana.

"We have Silver Streak saddled and ready to go for you," Emeline said, directing her comment to Solana. "She's not fond of male riders."

Solana smiled and hooked her thumb toward him. "Best not put this old bull rider on her then."

Adan twisted his lips as she nudged his shoulder. "I'm not that old."

"Not to worry," Cooper said. "Confetti is less picky. She enjoys a spirited ride."

Adan bit back a question about the "spirited ride," before holding out his hand for the mare to smell. She leaned closer, so he stroked her blaze and neck.

"Give us a minute and we'll get Optimus Prime tacked up."

Cooper whistled. Optimus trotted toward the barn while Jet ran alongside him with a grin revealing straight, even teeth.

"It's good to see him smile," Emeline said, kneading her low back. "Been a hard eighteen months for him."

"We hadn't realized she'd been sick for so long." Solana voiced the words he'd been thinking.

"Her boyfriend, Arturo, had just proposed the weekend before she learned she had cancer." Emeline's gaze darted to Jet. "She had been feeling off for a bit, but finally felt good enough for a weekend trip with Arturo. We had the pleasure of watching Jet and being the first to learn about their engagement. She came back glowing, excited for their future. Jet had grown close to Arturo, too."

Adan kicked the toe of his boot on the ground, frustrated by the news. Guess Jet lost more than his mama. Wonder what happened to Arturo.

Emeline sniffed before she continued. "Then, out of nowhere, she ended up in the hospital. Stage four cancer. They gave her six months." Emeline snorted. "'Course it was just like Annabel to prove them wrong and fight hard to stick around longer."

Adan swallowed back the growing lump in his throat. "What happened to Arturo?"

"Oh, he tried to take care of Annabel. Tried to get her to marry him despite her prognosis. Saying he wanted whatever time she had left and that Jet would need a father. The more he pressed, the more stubborn she became. She broke off the engagement and told him to find someone else."

Solana sucked in a sharp breath. Adan squeezed her hand, surprised to find he held it again without realizing it. Sounded like Annabel's stubborn streak survived to the end.

Emeline met his gaze as Cooper led Optimus Prime out of the stable with Jet perched on top. With a gentle lean, Jet reached out to pat his horse's neck, clearly enjoying the reunion with his steed. It warmed Adan's heart to see a glimmer of happiness on his son's face.

"Arturo is a good man. She broke his heart and Jet's by calling it off. I sure hope she knew what she was doing."

Concern resonated in Emeline's voice, and Adan couldn't help but notice. Without a doubt, she questioned what qualities made him more suitable to be Jet's father than Arturo. Truthfully, he wondered the same.

"Come on, Adan! Solana! Let's ride!"

Jet's posture in the saddle remained tall as the light in his eyes brightened his entire being. Relief filled Adan at having gotten one thing right. His son needed this outing. Maybe he could navigate this fatherhood thing after all.

"I BROUGHT SOME trail snacks and beverages," Solana said to Emeline as Adan untied the saddled horses.

"Coop! You got a saddlebag on Confetti?"

"Sure thing, darling."

"You can put your things in that."

With a grateful smile, Solana thanked Emeline and quickly retrieved the bag from the truck, eager to continue their day. After arming it, Adan packed the saddlebags with the food and drink. He offered to give her a leg up, and she contemplated whether it was a deliberate gesture meant specifically for her or a habit from years of leading trail rides back home.

"Lanni?"

She stirred from her thoughts and accepted his help, even though she could have mounted on her own. Once she settled in, he adjusted the stirrups for her before mounting Confetti. The sable horse side stepped until Adan adjusted his hold on the reins.

"Jet, you familiar with the trails?" he asked.

"Yeah."

"Why don't you lead?"

Jet turned Optimus toward a trail that meandered behind the barn toward a wash. As Solana nudged Silver Streak forward, she noticed Adan's strange look.

"What? I got some dirt on my face or something?"

Adan chuckled. "Just realized this is our first horse ride together. And how incredible you look on top of a horse, cowgirl."

Solana's cheeks flamed, but she managed a barb. "Well, our first horse ride could have been ages ago, if you'd only asked."

Instead of the laughter she expected, he sobered. "You're right. I should have asked you years ago. Should have..."

He maneuvered Confetti next to her as the trail widened. His serious expression and sincere eyes sent tingles radiating through her. She liked this new side of him.

"Given all that's happened in the last week... Lanni, I've been a complete idiot. I should have pursued a relationship long before now. I've wasted so many years."

Solana bit the inside of her lip when he lowered his voice. "What happened to Arturo could have happened to me. I could have missed out—"

"Adan! Can we take the long way?"

Ugh. Sure felt like he had been about to confess something really important. Like maybe that he liked her? Loved her?

Solana slowly exhaled as Adan joined Jet at the fork, asking questions about each trail.

Though Jet wormed his way into her heart, his interruption annoyed her. She had waited years—many, many years—for Adan to show any interest in her. From what he had been saying, it sounded like he hid his feelings from her nearly as long as she'd hidden hers from him.

"What do you say, Lanni? Scenic ascending trail with a view overlooking the valley or dry bed of a river?"

"Scenic view."

"Lead the way, Jet."

Jet fist pumped the air before guiding Optimus Prime to the high trail. She followed behind on Silver Streak as Adan brought up the rear. Soon, the trail narrowed, forcing Solana to focus solely on the path ahead. She couldn't help but feel a tinge of disappointment, longing for a moment alone with Adan to address his cryptic remark. With a sigh, she resigned herself to matching the steady pace set by the preteen, aware of Adan's gaze lingering on her back.

As the trail leveled out, a vast plateau unfurled in front of them, adorned with clusters of petite trees and brush, reminiscent of the scenery surrounding Vargas Ranch. With a tranquil exhale, she shut her eyes and angled her face towards the sun, basking in its soothing rays that brought solace to her spirit. She could have spent her vacation sunning herself on a crowded beach in Cabo, pining for home. Instead, Solana relished the time with Adan and Jet. They felt almost like a family.

Adan trotted up next to her as she soaked in nature's serenity.

"What a view," she murmured.

"Couldn't agree more."

She turned, captivated by the deep, husky timbre of Adan's voice, resonating in her ears like a velvety melody. As his piercing eyes grazed over her face, a magnetic energy enveloped them, drawing them closer together emotionally. The intensity between them was palpable, amplifying the love she felt for him. A rush of heat flushed her cheeks, causing a tingling sensation to spread across her skin. She moistened her dry lips before she finally spoke.

"Might be good to stop for a break."

Solana felt Adan's gaze remain on her while he called out to Jet to wait up. When they reached him, Adan dismounted and offered her a hand, but she declined. The leather creaked as she slowly lowered from the saddle. Her legs, unsteady, wobbled like gelatin, a reminder of how long it'd been since her last ride.

Adan tied his horse before reaching for her reins and tying off hers. Then she retrieved the snacks and beverages. After handing some to Jet, she sank to the ground and sat cross-legged.

"How much further does the trail go?" she asked.

Jet answered, "Another mile before it curves around the mountain back to the ranch. Mama, Arturo, and I rode it a lot."

Solana silently prayed for him, noticing the glassiness in his eyes. He bit off a chunk of the string cheese, bringing a smile to her face.

"You and your odd way to eat string cheese," she teased.

Adan chuckled. "Never tried it that way."

He chewed off a hunk of his instead of pulling it apart.

"Good thing you're pretty." She nudged his arm.

"You would love me, anyway."

Oh, if he only knew how much truth filled those words.

As their gazes tangled, a wave of anticipation coursed through her veins, causing her heart to beat faster and her breath to quicken. Solana felt a gentle heat rising in her cheeks. The surrounding air seemed charged with electricity and every nerve in her body seemed to come alive, as if tiny sparks of energy danced beneath her skin. In that long moment of locked gazes, their emotional worlds collided, leaving her breathless.

With a stuttered breath, Jet launched to his feet, swiftly wiping his face with his arm. He scurried toward his horse, tossing the rest of his uneaten snack on the ground.

Crud. Instead of getting caught up in Adan, she should have focused on the boy's pain and helping him through it.

"I'll go after him."

She stood and started toward the horses as Jet mounted Optimus and kicked him to a gallop.

"Lanni, it's not your responsibility."

Mounting Silver Streak, Solana ignored Adan, urging the mare to speed up, leaving him far behind. Sensing her pursuit, Jet tucked closer to Optimus' neck, propelling the horse forward with the grace of a thoroughbred. The thundering of hooves drowned out other sounds as she pursued the emotional boy. Silver Streak's sides heaved, reminding her of the horse's age. Concerned, she gradually decreased the pace to a trot.

She turned in her saddle as she heard Adan's horse galloping behind her. He slowed the horse when he caught up to her. Confetti snorted and pranced while Adan tried to hold her still enough to ask, "Which way?"

Solana pointed toward the last direction she saw Jet ride. Scanning the horizon, she could no longer make out his horse.

Adan's voice echoed through the expanse as he hollered at his horse, the sound carrying back to her on the breeze. Gripping the reins tightly, he dug his heels into Confetti's sides. With a burst of energy, the mare surged forward, her hooves pounding the ground, creating a symphony of rhythmic thuds. The air filled with the scent of kicked-up dust, swirling in their wake.

Solana's shoulders drooped as she watched helplessly before slowing Silver Streak to a walk.

Good one, Solana. She was supposed to be there to comfort Jet—to be the one in tune with the grieving child's emotions. She couldn't believe she'd been so distracted by Adan and their growing affection that she missed the signs of Jet's grief. After he mentioned his mama and Arturo, she should have paid more attention and asked him questions.

Solana continued forward at a walk, allowing Silver Streak to cool down and catch her breath. Hopefully, Adan would find Jet soon. And maybe he'd forget about her lack of motherly instincts.

9

ADAN'S STOMACH ROILED, threatening to toss up the string cheese as he watched his son speed away from them. He worried Jet's emotions would blind him to good horsemanship. He was only twelve years old. Even if he'd been riding for years, Adan doubted Jet would be as careful as he should. Could injure himself or the horse.

He pushed off the ground, knee popping loudly as he watched Solana take off after Jet. At least she would be sensible.

Adan shook off the stiffness in his leg and jogged to his horse, stuffing the remnants of their hurried snack into the saddlebags. Then he mounted Confetti and pushed her hard. As he closed in on Solana, she gently slowed down Annabel's older barrel racing horse to a trot. He paused long enough to ask her what direction Jet took before searching for his son.

Lord, please keep him safe. Help him ride smart.

With a growing sense of dread, Adan anxiously scanned the vast horizon, straining his eyes to glimpse Jet. As his gaze traveled across the landscape, a solitary hill emerged, breaking the monotony of the flat plateau. Perhaps Jet had ventured around it, Adan thought, his heart racing.

With a determined resolve, he urged the spirited mare forward, her powerful muscles propelling them towards the hill. As they galloped with increasing speed, the gusts of wind enveloped them, causing the mare's long mane to whip wildly in the air. The wind howled in his ears, and the steady beat of Confetti's hooves echoed in his chest, reverberating with an intensity matching the pounding of his own heart. His anxiety pressed heavily on him.

Hopefully, Solana would follow the trail around the mountain, finding her way back to the ranch. The last thing he needed was to lose both of them.

A plume of fine dust billowed into the air, swirling in tiny particles that danced in the sunlight. Adan adjusted his trajectory to catch up to Jet. The horse beneath him moved swiftly, unperturbed by the bumpy ride. Her frenetic pace brought Adan closer to his destination, the adrenaline coursing through his veins heightening his senses. He must find his son.

Suddenly, a deafening sound pierced the air as Optimus reared up in a display of raw power. Adan's eyes widened in horror as he watched his son tumble over the horse's back, the impact cracking his small body against the hard ground. The sight sent a chill down Adan's spine, and his muscles tensed with fear as a rattler slithered off the trail away from his son.

His grip on the reins tightened, causing them to creak under the pressure. The smell of leather and sweat filled his nostrils as he pulled back, urging Confetti to slow down, her hooves skidding on the dusty trail. Optimus, a blur in the distance, rushed off, leaving them behind.

With a hasty motion, Adan swung his leg over Confetti's back, his feet hitting the dirt with a thud. He dropped to his knees next to Jet's motionless form, the rough texture of the trail digging into his skin through his jeans. The smell of earth surrounded him, mingling with the scent of fear hanging in the air.

"Lord, please," Adan whispered, his voice barely audible amidst the chaos of his racing thoughts. His fingers, trembling with a mix of desperation and hope, reached for

Jet's pulse, feeling the steady rhythm of life beneath his touch. Relief washed over him like a gentle breeze, causing his tense shoulders to relax.

His hands moved with urgency, his touch gentle yet firm, as he checked Jet's limbs, head, neck, and chest for any signs of injury. The sound of his racing heartbeat filled his ears, drowning out the world around him. And then, like a sweet melody, a soft moan escaped Jet's lips as he pulled himself upright, his movements filled with pain.

"My head hurts."

Adan clutched the frail boy against his chest. He ran his hand over his head again, noticing the lump forming on his skull.

"Let's get you back to the ranch."

He carried Jet to Confetti, lifting the boy into the saddle. Then he mounted behind him. Once settled, Jet leaned against him, turning his face into Adan's chest.

"Where's Optimus?"

Adan ignored the question as he debated whether to turn around or continue forward. He slid his phone from his shirt pocket. No signal. Of course not. Gotta love country living.

Jet clenched a fistful of his shirt as he sucked in a sharp breath. "Everything hurts."

Laying the reins against Confetti's neck, Adan pointed her back the way they had come. He gently murmured reassuring sounds to his son, his heart filling with a newfound sense of protectiveness. He understood he had to be strong, to guide and teach his son, and to provide the security he needed. But the raw emotion he felt for his son after a few days startled him.

As much as he wanted to rush back to the Lazy D, he kept the horse at a walk. In a few minutes, they met Solana on the trail.

"What happened?"

"Optimus Prime threw him. Hit his head."

Jet snuffled, and Adan felt the tears soaking through his shirt. "I want. My. Mama."

Adan's eyes stung as he laid his palm flat, rubbing circles on his son's back. He swallowed down the dryness in his throat.

"You got any bars on your phone?"

Solana retrieved it and checked. "Yeah. One."

"Can you text Cooper to let him know Jet was thrown? He might have a concussion. And Optimus ran away."

"On it."

As her fingers flew across the screen, Adan's shoulders bunched. What a mess. They were on an unfamiliar trail on a stranger's ranch and he was holding his hurting son he'd only met a few days ago. He needed to get him to the hospital.

In a few minutes, a ping sounded. Solana read the incoming text. "Cooper says he'll send a ranch hand out to find Optimus."

Jet's breath shuddered before his words filled with sorrow. "I'm sorry. I hope he'll be okay."

"Don't worry," Adan whispered. "He's a smart horse. Cooper's cowboys won't stop until they find him."

"He also said they've called an ambulance. If you want to ride on ahead, give me your keys and I'll meet you at the hospital. Just let me know what one."

Again, Solana's selfless service stirred him. When life settled down, he would find some way to thank her. He pressed his keys into her hand before leaving her in his dust. At least he wouldn't have to worry about her finding her way back. He trusted Cooper to make sure she'd be alright too.

Before they arrived at the trailhead, paramedics found them on the trail. They examined Jet and strapped him to a special gurney used for the rough terrain. They continued to monitor his vitals on the excruciatingly slow walk back to the parking lot.

As soon as they arrived, Adan dismounted, tossing the

reins over a rail. Then he joined Jet in the back of the ambulance. The sturdy vehicle jostled over the uneven drive. When the tires hit the pavement, loud sirens blared overhead, sending a chill down Adan's spine. Jet faded in and out of consciousness on the ride to the hospital.

Lord, please let him be alright.

SOLANA SWIPED AT the tears moistening her cheeks, watching Adan ride off with his injured son. *Lord, calm them both. Help the paramedics and doctors know what to do. Heal Jet.*

She inhaled, straightening her spine, and breathed out. Silver Streak plodded along the trail, recovered from the hard ride. When she heard the sirens in the distance, the guilt pelted her heart. If only she had noticed Jet's emotional state. Maybe she could have offered him comfort and helped him deal with his pain.

But she hadn't noticed.

Please let Adan forgive me for letting his son get hurt.

Horse hooves thundered toward her, kicking up dust in the distance, pulling her from her condemning thoughts. As they grew nearer, they slowed. One cowboy stopped to ask her what happened. She shared the brief story, and the last known area Adan had seen Optimus Prime. When the conversation ended, they rode out to find Jet's horse.

Not long afterwards, she arrived at the Lazy D stables. Cooper took her horse before handing her a bag with the items Adan left behind.

"Solana, wait!" Emeline called as she hurried toward to her. "Can we take a minute to pray?"

She nodded, grateful for the woman's concern.

"Lord Jesus, we ask for your covering. Keep Solana safe as she drives to the hospital. Mend Jet's body, mind, and soul. Help him recognize You during this stormy season.

Bring peace to Adan and Solana as they care for him. Let this bond them together as a family."

"Amen." Cooper's confident voice ended the prayer.

"We'll keep praying for you. And if it's not too much trouble, let us know how he's doing."

"Will do," Solana tossed over her shoulder as she sprinted to Adan's truck.

Swinging the heavy door open, she climbed behind the wheel, scooted the seat forward, and turned on the engine. She anxiously searched for the text from Adan with the hospital's name and directions. Then she drove like the wind, praying the entire way.

As tears threatened to escape, Solana swallowed them down, stunned by the depth of her connection to Jet. She cared for him deeply. He was becoming the son of her heart.

Only she wasn't his mom. Would never be his stepmom. Regardless of Emeline's impression, they weren't a family. No, Solana was a lovesick fool yearning for a man going through a major life change. The closeness she felt with him—that kiss—it couldn't be trusted. She must distance herself. Get back to Wickenburg before she lost her heart to both of them.

Turning into a parking spot at the hospital, she jammed the shifter into Park. Then she scooted the seat back to where she thought it had been before sliding off the seat. The door closed with a soft thud, representing how she must close her heart.

Going to Albuquerque with Adan had been a mistake, Solana admitted, her father's admonition echoing in her mind. She had allowed her emotions to overpower her rationality, craving Adan's attention above all else. Now, her heart paid the price. Not only had her love for Adan deepened, but she also cared for his son in a way that only Adan's future wife should. It wasn't right for her, a mere platonic friend, to know his secret.

Except there was nothing platonic about his kiss. Or him

holding hands with her. Touching her shoulder. Hugging her. Making heart-eyes at each other. Something had sparked, turning into a smoldering ember, threatening to choke the oxygen from her lungs with a lone thought. Her heart belonged to Adan in a way she couldn't undo, but for her own sake, she had to try.

10

ADAN STARED AT his phone while doctors attended his son in another room. Scrolling through his contacts, his thumb hovered over Dylan's name. They had been friends for decades and brothers in the few years since Dylan married Adan's younger sister, Brisa.

He frowned. He hadn't told him about Jet. Only told him he needed some time off. At some point, he had stopped confiding in Dylan. Probably when he had grown closer to Lanni.

Before he could change his mind, he pressed Dylan's name and held the phone to his ear.

"Adan. Everything okay?"

The sound of his best friend's voice brought a wave of comfort he desperately needed. Adan cleared his throat.

"I'm at the hospital in Albuquerque. My son was thrown from his horse."

"Is he alright?"

"Not sure. He's in with the doctors. They're checking him for a concussion."

Dylan started praying right there with him on the phone. An occasional stutter showed his friend empathized with Adan's situation. Probably thinking what he'd do if it had been his son Braden.

As Dylan ended the prayer, Adan felt a whisper-soft peace begin to wrap around his soul. Jet would be alright.

God was still in control and had not abandoned them.

"So… Your son?"

Adan wiped a hand over his face. "His name is Jet. He's twelve."

"Hmm. From your rodeo days."

"Yeah. It's a long story. His mama died from cancer and never told me about him."

"That must be hard."

Adan nodded. "It is. We're adapting. And Solana has been a tremendous help."

"She went with you?"

Adan stood and paced the length of the nearly empty waiting room. It surprised him Dylan didn't know.

"I mean, Rennie said Solana was on vacation. Not that she…"

"She's helping me pack up Annabel's house."

A brief memory of their kiss caused heat to warm Adan's face. No way would he tell Dylan about that, especially not with how poorly Adan had reacted years ago when he learned Dylan fell for Brisa.

"She's always had the gift of service," Dylan said. "She spent days with Mami going through our grandfather's things when he passed a few years ago. I'm glad you're not walking through this alone."

A noise came from the background, and Dylan's voice softened. "Hey, I've gotta go. Brisa and I will pray for all of you."

The line went dead, so Adan tucked his phone into his pocket.

"Mr. Garrison?"

Adan whirled to face the male nurse, glancing at his name tag. "Tom, I'm Jet's dad. Adan Franco."

The man's dark eyes rounded. "Weren't you a Pro Bull Riding World Champion?"

His gut twisted as he imagined what the nurse must be thinking. "Yup. How's my son?"

Tom stared for a few seconds before shaking his head, muttering to himself. Adan sighed. Great. A new odd reaction to being recognized… With a son.

"Jet?" he prompted the nurse.

"He's in room 206. You can see him now. The doctor will be in shortly."

Adan found the room and leaned in. The sight of Jet sent the muscles in his shoulders coiling. He looked pale and tiny, propped up against the pillow. Wires and monitors were all over his arms. The worst part? His haunted, red-rimmed eyes. *Lord, give me wisdom to know what to say and do.*

"Hey, bud."

Jet's lower lip quivered. Adan rushed to his side, placing his large hand over his son's small one. Rubbing his thumb over the boy's knuckles, he waited silently. Tears leaked from Jet's eyes.

"You hurting?"

"No, sir."

"Hey, I thought we agreed you could call me Adan."

Jet's chin dropped to touch his chest.

"Jet. Look at me." Adan leaned over, tenderly brushing Jet's hair out of his eyes. "I will always be here for you. I promise."

When his son's eyes squeezed shut and his shoulders shook, Adan prayed he hadn't said the wrong thing.

"That's what. Mama said."

Crud.

Adan scooted a chair up to Jet's bedside. "I know, bud. And she did her best to live up to that promise. But you're right. Some things are out of our control. So, as long as I'm able, I will be here for you. 'Kay?"

Jet tried to dry his face, but the hospital wires made it difficult. Adan grabbed a few tissues and handed them to him.

A soft feminine throat cleared from the doorway, causing Adan's attention to shift.

"Mr. Garrison?"

Adan bit back the reminder of the truth that Jet wasn't really his. He refused to dwell on it. God brought him into Jet's life to be his dad, and his heart had accepted the assignment.

"Adan Franco. Jet's dad."

The diminutive Asian woman nodded sharply. "Doctor Nguyen. We ran some tests and everything looks good. No signs of a concussion or internal damage." She crossed the room and clasped Jet's hand. "You are one lucky young man." Then her gaze flitted to Adan. "No broken bones either. We'd like to keep him here for an hour as a precaution."

"Thank you, doctor."

She withdrew her hand and left the room.

"Thank you, Lord," Adan whispered. "Sounds like you're gonna be just fine."

Jet shrugged and looked away.

Adan swiped a hand over his face and beard before easing into the chair. He turned on the TV before switching to the Disney channel. He had no idea what Jet liked, but sensed his son's desire not to talk.

He retrieved his phone and scrolled through the dozens of missed messages. One from Dylan reminding him they were praying for him. Two from Solana. She had left the ranch. A second saying she'd arrived at the hospital. Cooper Dunbar's cowboy found Optimus.

"Looks like they found your horse."

"Is he alright?"

"Yeah. Cooper says they are spoiling him with a massage and extra treats. He'll be just fine. He thinks a snake on the trail spooked Optimus."

While Jet watched TV, Adan returned to his phone. He texted an update to his mama, who quickly replied that she and Dad were praying.

He felt incredibly blessed by the number of friends and

family that texted him. Some who he hadn't told directly. Peace wrapped him in an embrace. He wouldn't be alone raising Jet.

Solana still hadn't shown up, despite the text from nearly a half hour ago that she had arrived. Maybe the nurses wouldn't let her back.

"I'm gonna see what is keeping Solana. I'll be back in a second."

He walked down to the nurses' station. Not seeing her, he continued on to the cafeteria, craving a coffee. He purchased one before searching the large space for Solana. Still not finding her, he grew concerned.

A MALE NURSE'S voice floated toward Solana long before she arrived at the nurses' station.

"You were right. It is Adan Franco, the PBR World Champion."

"Who's he here to see?" a high-pitched female voice asked.

"His kid."

"There's no Franco on the board."

The male nurse responded. "Kid's last name is Garrison."

Solana crept toward the counter, staying out of sight as long as she could. A blond curly haired woman, the owner of the high-pitched voice, gasped.

"I thought he was a Christian."

"Netty, he could have become a Christian after the kid was born," said a voluptuous woman as her fingernails clacked against the keyboard in front of her.

"Doubt it."

Just then, the male nurse—Tom, according to his name tag—spotted Solana. "Can we help you?"

"I'm looking for Jet Garrison."

Netty glared at her, causing her face to heat. They probably thought she was the woman who birthed the famous bull rider's kid out of wedlock. Great.

The bigger nurse looked up from the computer. "Just down the hall, take a right, then a left."

"Thanks."

As Solana walked away, she heard Netty murmur. "Buckle bunny." Followed by a "What? She totally looks like she could be."

The comment sliced through her. Why did people like Netty feel the need to express their opinions on subjects they knew nothing about?

Straightening her back, Solana counted to five outside Jet's door. She exhaled and smiled before stepping into the room. Her smile faltered when she did not spot Adan.

"Hey, Jet."

"Hey."

She crossed the room and leaned over, placing a kiss on his forehead. Ugh. Why had she done that? She wasn't his mom. Just his dad's friend. A friend he would forget all about once the busyness of life returned to normal, and he raised Jet on his own.

"How are you feeling?"

"Okay."

"Any major damage?"

Jet shook his head.

"None." Adan's voice came from behind her.

She whirled around to face him. He stood closer than she expected. When he reached for her hand, she feigned the need to finger comb her hair. She couldn't let him keep acting like a couple. Not if she wanted to spare herself future heartbreak.

"The doctor said we should be able to leave soon. No broken bones. No concussion. She recommended some pain relievers and rest. Probably gonna be sore for a day or two."

"Mr. Franco?" Tom said from the doorway. "We just need to confirm the insurance details and get your signature on the discharge paperwork. Lawanda will help you down at the counter while I get Jet ready."

Adan dropped his head back and looked at the ceiling. "I haven't added him to my insurance yet."

Solana stretched her hand toward him, but withdrew it quickly. "You can add him when we get back home. I remember Rennie saying you have thirty days after a qualifying event to make changes. I'm sure this counts."

Adan offered a half smile before letting Jet know he'd be right back. Then he left the room.

"Okay, buddy. Let's get all this stuff off you." Tom chatted with Jet doing a great job distracting him while he removed all the wires and such. Then he handed Jet a bag and asked him to change in the bathroom. "Your mom can help—"

Jet's chin trembled. "My mama is dead."

Tom's eyes rounded as he raised an eyebrow at Solana. She helped Jet from the bed, squeezing his shoulder.

"You need any help?"

Jet shook his head. Once he was in the bathroom, Solana pivoted toward the nurse.

"His mom died of cancer a couple of weeks ago."

"Oh, I'm so sorry. So, so sorry."

Tom hurried from the room as she tried to calm her fury. His assumption seemed natural, given the circumstances. She shouldn't hold a grudge, even if her protectiveness flared.

She inventoried the room for any personal items of Jet's or Adan's. Seeing none, she waited for Jet to finish dressing. When he entered the room, she took the bag his clothes had been in and tossed it in the trash. Then she walked with him to find Adan.

Adan glanced at her before he finished signing the paperwork. "All done?"

"Yep. You're free to go," Lawanda said, offering a kind smile. "You take care, young man." She waved a warning finger at Jet. "No more falling off your horse."

Jet ducked behind Solana and out of view of the woman. Adan placed a hand on Jet's shoulder and guided him toward the exit. Solana followed along.

She leaned closer to Adan to ask if he'd heard anything about Optimus.

"Yeah. Cooper said they found him. He's good."

Relief washed over her as she created a little space between her and Adan.

"Where'd you park?"

Warmth spread across her cheeks. "This way."

Solana marched toward the truck, only slowing when she spotted it. She disarmed it before tossing Adan the keys. After Jet settled in the back, she climbed into the passenger seat, crossing her arms.

As Adan drove back to Annabel's house, Solana stewed. Despite her enduring love for him and her desire to become his wife, she reluctantly understood that creating distance between them was the right course of action. No matter how painful, it was necessary for his sake. He needed the space and time to adjust to being a father and to build a strong bond with Jet without the distraction of her presence.

She angled her face toward the window, allowing a few tears to trail down her cheeks, giving into the sorrow of her soul. It would all be easier once they were back home. She would be busy with work and Adan would be busy buying a house and taking care of his son.

So if it was the right thing, why did it hurt so much?

11

As Adan walked into Annabel's church the next morning, he resisted the urge to hold Solana's hand. The pull toward her intensified the more she distanced herself from him. Ever since the ride home from the hospital, she had withdrawn. She had said little during supper. As soon as they finished, she hid out in the guest room to read.

His heart squeezed tight as he placed his hand on Jet's shoulder. It would be easier to face these people — Annabel's church family — with Solana's comforting touch. Holding her hand had become a habit he sorely missed in less than a day.

"Arturo!"

Jet shrugged off Adan's hand and darted down the aisle toward a Mexican man with a kind smile. The man held his arms wide for Jet, causing Adan's stomach to sink. What made him a better candidate to be Jet's father than Arturo?

Annabel's wishes.

A small part of him regretted burning her letter. He might need reminding now and again.

Adan squared his shoulders and pasted on the most genuine smile he could muster under the circumstances. Holding his hand out in greeting, he said, "I'm Adan Franco, Jet's dad."

"Pleasure to meet you." Arturo's smile faded, and his eyes narrowed slightly, contradicting his words. Fair enough. Had their roles been reversed, Adan might have felt the same.

"Hi," Solana said before she introduced herself as Adan's friend.

He bit back a sigh as Arturo greeted her far more warmly. Solana offered the man condolences as more people milled around them.

Jet stood next to Arturo, looking up at him with anticipation. Arturo asked Jet how he was holding up. Their voices lowered, and Adan refused to insert himself into their conversation. He was grateful that Emeline had told him about Arturo and Annabel's relationship the previous day.

Adan's stomach churned, and he tried to unpack his anxiety. Seeing Arturo and Jet together like father and son spawned a host of insecurities inside Adan. They had history. Planned to become a family. He could let that happen. All he had to do was request a paternity test. Surely, the courts would allow Arturo to adopt Jet if Adan didn't stand in his way.

But Annabel. She broke things off with Arturo, knowing she neared the end of her life. If she wanted Arturo to be Jet's dad, all she had to do was to marry him and push through the adoption papers before she died.

She had done none of it. Instead, she penned a letter to Adan, the man she knew from her rodeo days confessing what she'd done. She had asked him to raise her son.

None of it made sense. It never would. Annabel took her reasoning to her grave.

"You must be Adan," a fifty-something woman greeted him.

"Yes," he replied, glancing at Jet periodically. Solana whispered something to him and he took off toward a hall of rooms.

"I'm Edward Haynes' wife, Susan."

He brightened and shook her hand before introducing Solana.

"How is Jet adjusting?" She directed the question to

Solana.

"As well as expected. Thank you so much for stocking the fridge and for that delicious casserole."

Adan cleared his throat. "Yes, thank you. It was a tremendous relief to have food on hand when we arrived."

"Of course. We just loved Annabel and would do anything for her. Jet is fortunate to have you both in his life." Susan squeezed his arm. "Well, service is about to start. Best find my Edward."

Adan stepped aside so Solana could enter the row of padded chairs. Then he sat next to her, resting his arm on the seatback behind her.

"Where'd Jet go?" he asked.

"To the youth group." She squirmed in her seat. "Do you mind?" She nodded toward his arm. "I don't want more people to think…"

Disappointment crashed over his heart as Adan returned his arm to his side. Something caused Lanni to retreat from him, and he hated it. Maybe someone said something about them being a family. He wouldn't mind if that became reality. Maybe she did. Maybe he'd read her reaction to his kiss wrong.

When the lights dimmed for the service, Adan forced his attention away from Lanni and towards worshipping God. The band played several songs, including a few he knew. He closed his eyes when one particular song spoke to his soul. The song transitioned into an old hymn. *It is well with my soul.*

Despite the turmoil and rapid changes of the last week, Adan could confidently sing those words. His soul was just fine. God was still in control. And He had a plan for Adan, Jet, and even Solana. He needed to trust God with his doubts.

When the service ended, Jet skidded to a stop in front of Adan.

"Can I go over to Zack's house? Please, please, please?"

"Introduce me to his parents first."

Jet tugged on Adan's arm and dragged him over to a petite brunette. "This is—"

"Chrissy Delacroix?" Her name dropped from Adan's lips before he pulled her into a hug.

"Adan Franco." A frown flitted from her features before she offered a tentative smile. "Fancy seeing you here. And with Jet."

"Lanni, come meet Chrissy."

As he introduced Solana, he noticed the tenseness in her smile. Wonder what that was about.

"Chrissy was a champion team roper back in the day."

"Nice to meet you," Solana said.

"So I guess Jet knows your son?"

Chrissy narrowed her eyes briefly. "They are best friends." She let out a gusty breath. "Can we talk for a minute?"

"Sure."

Adan followed her lead as she walked a few paces away from the boys and lowered her voice.

"Can't say that I pictured you being Jet's father."

Heat warmed his face as the truth niggled. "Well, turns out I am. Though I'm sorry Annabel never told me. I would have been involved in his life, had I known."

"Hmm. I believe that part is true. I thought you were only friends."

Adan shrugged. "Guess you thought wrong."

Chrissy frowned. He watched the way her expression changed with each thought running through her mind. At last, she continued. "You're gonna take Jet to Arizona, aren't you?"

"It's where I live and work."

When Chrissy nodded slowly, his chest tightened. "I figured. You mind if Jet hangs out with us this afternoon? Give him and Zack a chance for their goodbyes?"

Adan's heart ached for his son again. Another loss for

the boy. He tucked away the thought of making sure the boys stayed connected over video chats. Maybe he would invite Zack and his mom out to the ranch for a week during a school break.

"Yeah, I think that'd be good for them both." Adan rubbed a hand over the back of his neck. "Looks like I'll need your contact info and address to pick him up."

They exchanged numbers.

"Thanks, Adan. This will mean more than you know to the boys."

"Guess you and Annabel kept in touch all these years."

Chrissy snorted before quickly wiping away a glare. "We did. Our boys were born a few months apart. Both of us are… Were… Single moms. We relied on each other. I'm gonna miss her as much as Zack and I will miss Jet."

"We'll make sure they keep in touch."

She followed him back to where the boys stood next to Solana.

"Alright, Jet. You can go to the Delacroix's for the afternoon. I want you to have Chrissy call me if you aren't feeling well." Adan shifted his gaze to Chrissy. "His horse threw him yesterday. No broken bones or concussion, but let me know…"

"I will. Thanks again, Adan."

He felt all kinds of awkward leaving Jet with her, even if she wasn't a complete stranger. Guess if Annabel had trusted her, he ought to as well.

"See you in a few hours." He tousled Jet's hair before ushering Solana toward his truck.

"Someone else from your past?"

He bristled at her tone. "Yeah, I knew Chrissy in the rodeo. She's good people." Or she had been then. Probably still was given she went to Annabel's church.

"Huh."

Solana's wary expression caught Adan's attention before she averted her eyes and looked out the window. The change in her since Jet's accident the day before bothered him. She'd erected a wall between them, and he didn't like it one bit.

"Mind if we stop for some fast food on the way back?" she asked.

They discussed options before he found something. Once back at Annabel's, Adan turned on a football game. Solana scarfed down her meal and disappeared into the guest room, leaving him feeling empty and alone.

SOLANA FLOPPED DOWN on the guest bed after closing the door. The sound of the football game dimmed. She wished she could talk to Rennie or her parents to sort through her jumbled feelings. They would be at Dalton's house for family dinner and that usually lasted several hours, especially if the men put on the game. She glanced at the weather for back home. A perfect day. The women probably sat outside on the back patio watching the kids play.

She'd only been gone a few days and missed her entire family. Each of her cousins' personalities was so diverse. Responsible Dalton, the oldest. Shy Dylan — though with his stutter, she couldn't fault him for that. Bossy, yet softening, Derin. A smile stretched across her face. Madison had a knack for gently smoothing out his rough edges. Even his little boy, Maverick, kept him on his toes.

Devon and Raina would be present, along with their adopted daughter Felipa. Such a tight-knit family. With Rennie's agreement to be their surrogate, Raina's dream of having a child would finally come true. They expected the baby to arrive in the following spring. The family dynamic would shift once more. By the time her sibling was born, Felipa would turn fourteen. Solana realized the age difference between Raina and her adopted daughter Felipa couldn't be much over ten years. That made her feel less uncomfortable about her own age difference from Jet.

Solana admired Rennie's sacrifice, but couldn't help worrying about the emotional toll it was taking. She had noticed a change in her sister's mood since being artificially inseminated with Devon and Raina's biological embryo. She took a few minutes from her reminiscing to pray for them all, but especially Rennie.

Candi and Drake would be at family dinner too, having married last Christmas. They were great together, and crazy in love. It would not surprise her to hear of a baby on the way soon.

Solana sighed. Yeah, she missed them all. Amazingly, not one of their family members had moved away from the area. Only Dad and Mom didn't work at the ranch. Everyone else did.

Her homesickness did little to distract her from the situation with Adan for long. Watching him hug Chrissy Delacroix sent her jealousy flaring again. Though, Chrissy seemed suspicious of Adan. Maybe Annabel had shared parts of her secret with her.

Solana rolled onto her back, staring at the white textured ceiling. They would finish boxing up the last things tomorrow. Then Adan would meet with Edward Haynes on Tuesday while Solana waited for the moving truck. By midafternoon, they ought to be headed back home. Only two more days of close quarters with Adan and his son.

When her eyes burned, she sat up. She loved both of them so much. Walking away from them on Tuesday night would devastate her. If only she could maintain a friendship with Adan. Maybe she could wall off the part of her heart that loved him and she could still be a part of their lives.

Her phone pinged, and she read the incoming text from her sister. Instead of responding, she started a video call.

"What's going on, Rennie?"

Her sister's eyes glistened, and she blinked rapidly.

"Raina is driving me crazy. Is there such a thing as a mom-to-be-zilla?"

Solana snorted. "Like a bridezilla? Maybe. What's she doing?"

Rennie sighed. "Only commenting about everything I ate. 'I read that spicy food isn't good for the baby.' You know, stuff like that."

"I'm sorry."

Rennie's shoulders sagged. "I know. I'm a horrible person. I get that I'm carrying her only biological child and that she really longs for the pregnancy experience that she'll never have. It's just she's driving me nuts."

"I'll say an extra prayer for you."

"Thanks. So, how's being stranded with Adan and his son?"

Solana rolled her eyes. "We're not stranded."

"You know, it's just like one of those 'forced proximity' romance novels you love."

"Yeah, no."

"Uh, oh. What happened?"

Before she thought better of it, Solana shared too much. "He kissed me."

Rennie's dark eyes rounded. "He what?"

"He kissed me the other night. Then we couldn't stop staring at each other for the better part of two days." Tears burned her eyes. "His son got thrown from his horse because I was a distraction."

"Somehow, I feel like that isn't true. Tell me more."

Solana relayed all the events from the last two days.

"Lanni, I think Adan is in love with you."

"Not anymore. Not after I caused his son's accident."

"Would you just stop? Listen to yourself. You caused nothing. And it's not your fault Jet galloped away on his horse or that his horse threw him. You aren't responsible for him. But even if you were, none of the blame rests on your shoulders."

Solana picked at the hem of her jeans.

"Lanni."

Finally, she expelled a loud breath. "You're probably right."

"I *am* right and you know it. I'm pretty sure Adan sees things clearly. Don't let false guilt come between you. Especially not after the first signs that he returns your feelings."

"Fine. You're right. But no, you cannot quote me on that."

Rennie smiled. "Thanks, Lanni. I'm glad you and I are friends. I've kinda missed you these last few days."

"Me too. Let's never live far apart, okay?"

"Deal."

A knock sounded on the door.

"I've got to go. Thanks, Rennie. I needed that. See you soon."

Solana hung up the phone and answered the door.

"Jet's ready to come home. I'm gonna pick him up. You wanna come along?"

"Sure. Maybe we can grab something for supper while we're out?"

Adan flashed her a grin. "I know just the place. Saw an ad for it during the game."

"Did the Cardinals win?"

Adan chortled. "Do they ever?"

"You got me there."

Solana grabbed her jacket and followed Adan to his truck. Before he opened the door for her, he touched her arm.

"What's wrong, Lanni?"

"Nothing." She lied as she reached for the handle.

His large hand covered hers. Then he gently turned her to face him.

"Something's been bugging you since yesterday." Adan tipped her face up toward him with a knuckle under her chin. "Tell me."

The musky scent uniquely him filled her senses. Everything within her longed for a deeply intimate and long-lasting relationship with him. How could it bloom if she failed to water it?

"I've been worried," she admitted. "That you blamed me for Jet taking off."

Adan shook his head as he dropped his hand to rest on her waist. "Far from it. He made a foolish choice yesterday. Neither one of us could have seen it coming."

When she dropped her gaze, he pulled her against his chest, wrapping his arms around her tenderly.

"Lanni," he whispered into her hair. "You've been so wonderful to us. Cooking. Packing. Sorting through someone else's stuff. Trying to draw Jet out and comfort him at the same time."

As the sun warmed her back, Solana leaned into his embrace, looping her arms around his waist. His solid form felt perfect against her. She nearly hummed when he unconsciously stroked a hand over the back of her head.

"I can't thank you enough for all that and more. Your wise advice and servant's heart have encouraged and supported us more than you'll ever know."

She leaned back slightly so she could look him in the eyes. "I just wanted to help him process some of his grief. Instead, I had been so wrapped up in this," she motioned a hand between them, "whatever it is, that I didn't pay attention like I should have."

A cloud blocked the sun's rays, causing Solana to shiver. Adan's face twisted. "If anyone failed, it was me. I'm Jet's dad. But I don't see that either of us failed. He's a twelve-year-old who just lost his mama after a long battle with cancer. He lost the man who he thought was gonna be his father. Then he was thrust upon a bunch of strangers who want to move him away from his church, his school, and his friends. It's gonna be a while before he figures it out."

Solana heard what Adan was saying.

"'Sides, didn't you say just the other day it was gonna take time and prayer for him to heal?"

"Yeah. Guess I did."

"See, you are the smart one. Your instincts are good."

She stepped back, then flicked her wrist to look at the date and time. "Mark that as when Adan Franco admitted I'm the brains of this friendship."

"That and so much more."

The husky quality of his voice sent shivers of delight down her spine. It also had her reaching for the truck handle.

"We better go pick him up."

"See, the smart one." He chuckled as he rounded the truck and slid behind the wheel.

Maybe she ought to go easier on herself. Seemed like Adan felt she helped a lot.

12

ON MONDAY EVENING, Adan stopped by Chrissy Delacroix's house. He had texted earlier, asking if she would mind returning Jet's school library books. As he parked along the street, Chrissy opened the door and stepped onto the porch, latching it behind her.

"Hey! Thanks for taking these back to the school." He thrust the grocery sack toward her.

She took the books, hugging them tightly against her middle.

"I, um, wanted to apologize for being so standoffish yesterday."

"No worries." He figured his sudden appearance at her church surprised her.

"You have a minute?"

The hair on the back of his neck stood on end at her unexpected request. He sat on the metal chair she motioned to. She eased onto the other one, setting the books on the small table between them. Chrissy's posture remained stiff as she looked anywhere but at him. Adan schooled his features, sensing this was no casual conversation.

"Annabel and I knew each other back in our rodeo days."

"I remember."

Chrissy bit her lip and several seconds ticked by.

"Look, I don't know how to explain all this. When you

showed up claiming to be Jet's dad... It threw me off. I didn't believe it. Still don't."

Adan leaned forward, bracing his elbows on his knees. "My name is on his birth certificate."

Chrissy snorted and met his gaze. "I believe you about that. But I don't think you are really Jet's father."

"Why's that?" He tried to keep the panic from his voice, wondering how close she and Annabel had been. And if Annabel had ever confided the truth. If she knew and sought legal action, it'd be her word against his. He probably had nothing to worry about. Good thing Annabel asked him to burn that letter. The only proof of anything in writing was his name on the birth certificate. Still didn't keep his heart rate from ticking up.

Chrissy glanced over her shoulder at the front window before continuing.

"The circumstances of how Annabel became pregnant match how I did, too."

Adan's throat constricted and his jaw twitched as he forced himself to remain perfectly still.

"I see by your reaction you know what I mean."

He nodded.

"And you and I both know you didn't father my son."

"Correct."

"I've long suspected that Zack and Jet are half-brothers. Born only a few months apart. The characteristics they share from their father are obvious to someone who knew him. Just a few differences inherited from their mothers."

Adan coughed into a fisted hand. "Did she tell you?"

"No. Only hinted around it. Made a comment once about them being brothers, which she quickly corrected to 'acting like brothers'. She knew who fathered Zack."

A chill ran down Adan's spine over this bizarre turn of events. "Why are you telling me this?"

Chrissy puffed her cheeks and blew out a breath as she sank against the back of the chair. "Sorry. I don't mean to cause you concern. I will say nothing to either of the boys. I know nothing for certain. However, I want them to remain close."

Adan scratched his bearded chin, relaxing in his seat. "We can make that happen. Weekly video chats. A visit to Vargas Ranch over school breaks." When she looked like she might object, he added, "I'll pay travel expenses."

"You don't have to do that. I'll figure it out. I think they would enjoy that."

Adan stood, hoping to bring the conversation to a close.

"Adan, I really appreciate you working with me on this."

He swallowed away any lingering fear. "Of course."

When he stepped off the porch, he turned back toward her.

"Chrissy? Do you know if Annabel had any family?"

"Her parents are both gone now. I think she had a brother who lived out of state. Never talked about getting together or staying in touch."

"Thanks. If you ever hear anything about family, please give them my contact info. I want Jet to know them if they're interested."

"Will do."

When he started toward the truck, she followed him.

"Adan, one more thing. I looked up what happened to… *Him.* He's in prison serving out several convictions for sexual assault. I have no intention of ever telling Zack, but just thought you might want to know."

He nodded and tossed out one more promise to keep the boys connected before driving away. His heart ached knowing that someone he had known from his rodeo days had caused such carnage to so many women's lives. At least the beast had been prosecuted. He wondered if Annabel had ever known.

Shaking off the heavy thoughts, he prayed for Chrissy and Zack Delacroix, asking God to bring them peace. Then he resolved to do everything in his power to help the boys remain best friends.

AS SOON AS Adan returned from the Delacroix's, Solana placed the heated store bought lasagna on the table along with some garlic bread. The savory aroma filled the dining area. It made for a convenient meal, given all the pots, pans, dishes, and silverware were packed in boxes.

Their last supper together. She sighed as she scooted in her chair, feeling far more sentimental than she expected.

Adan seemed in a solemn mood as he prayed for the meal. When he finished, he asked, "Jet, your room packed up?"

"Yes, Adan."

"Bathroom things too?"

Solana interjected, "I packed everything except what he'll need for his shower in the morning. I figured we could put the dirty towels and bed sheets in a garbage bag in the truck bed."

"Yeah. Sounds good."

Clean up from supper was a breeze. She tossed the leftovers, paper plates, and plastic ware into the trash.

Adan plopped down on the couch while Jet went to his room. When she entered the great room, Adan patted the spot next to him on the couch.

"I was going to read."

"Sit with me?"

His sad tone tugged at her heartstrings, so she cuddled against his side, reading her book. He looped an arm over her waist, careful not to disturb her reading. The remote in his other hand, he flipped through the channels, not landing on anything for too long.

"You're a surfer, huh?"

"What?"

She poked his arm. "A channel surfer."

"Not usually. Just have a lot on my mind."

Solana marked her place in the book and sat up, missing the weight of his arm around her. One of the many things she would miss when they returned to their normal lives.

"Tell me what's bugging you."

He glanced over his shoulder. "Jet's door closed?"

"Yeah."

"Chrissy told me she knows."

"What? How? Did Annabel tell her?"

"Not exactly. She said her son's father is the same man."

Solana's heart raced and her throat closed as her eyes burned. She shook her head.

"I know, Lanni. It's awful. Long story short, she doesn't want her son to know either, so the secret is safe."

"I can't believe it." She lowered her voice. "Are you saying her son is Jet's half-brother?"

"We think so."

"Oh, my. We have to invite them out on school breaks. Zack could spend the summer at my parents, or yours, or maybe you'll have space at your house—a spare room for him."

"All great ideas, Lanni. Both Chrissy and I are committed to supporting their friendship, no matter what."

She leaned back against him, rolling her lips inward as the reality of it all sank in. Adan rubbed his hand along her arm before looping his around her again.

"It's gonna be alright."

She shook her head. "How terrible."

"Chrissy said the man is in prison for his crimes. Seemed to help her."

"Good."

When the conversation ended, she returned to reading her book, trying to take her mind off the latest secret about Jet's life. She sure hoped they wouldn't learn about any more. A criminal for a father. An almost step-dad that Annabel pushed away. His best friend was really his half-brother. It overwhelmed her.

As much as Solana would miss living with Adan and Jet, she sure wouldn't miss the startling revelations about Annabel Garrison's life.

13

———

"I'M OFF," ADAN announced as he reached for his tan hat. "I'll bring some lunch back with me. What time are the movers coming again?"

"Ten."

His heart raced when Solana nudged his arm and pointed at herself. "Brains. Remember that."

He plopped his cowboy hat down on his head and pulled her into his arms before placing a kiss on her cheek.

"And pretty," he whispered as he released her. He waited one more second for the pink to color her cheeks before he scooted out the door.

As he climbed behind the wheel of his truck, a pang of sadness washed over him. He would miss seeing Solana every day. Miss waking up to her sloppy top knot and baggy pjs. Miss seeing her gorgeous smile before his first cup of coffee.

Adan forced himself to push away the images of her, focusing on the drive to the lawyer's office. Though Albuquerque seemed like a pleasant town, he couldn't wait to see it in his rearview mirror. He sure hoped he'd never have to close up an estranged friend's house again. And he prayed that Jet would someday understand the importance of relocating to Arizona.

Pulling into a parking space near the attorney's office building, he cut the engine. Once inside the quaint stucco building, Edward's secretary showed him to a conference room.

"Morning," Edward greeted him with a handshake. "I've got several forms for you to sign." He took a seat and fanned out the paperwork.

"This one grants me the authority to sell Annabel's house. We can keep the bank account open and add you to the account after we're finished here. That will allow you to transfer funds when everything is closed out."

"Sounds good."

Over the next hour, Edward had Adan sign many more papers transferring the ownership of the horses, the deed to the house, paperwork granting him control over a trust fund for Jet's education, and more. He even had to sign something allowing Edward to donate Annabel's car to a charity. By the time he tucked his readers into their case, his stomach growled.

Edward gave him directions to the bank before shaking his hand.

"If you have questions, please reach out. I'm here to assist in any way necessary."

"Thanks, Edward. And thank your wife again for us."

"Will do."

Adan headed over to the bank to sign papers to add him to the account. Then he stopped for sandwiches and chips at a sub shop before driving back to the house.

A medium-sized moving truck parked halfway in the driveway with a ramp extended towards the open garage. Two men carried the sofa from the living room up the ramp before returning to the house.

Adan walked through the front door. "Knock, knock."

"Hey, you're back."

Solana's smile sent waves of delight through his chest. He was really gonna miss that.

"I was about ready to call Haynes to see if you got lost."

"I'm starving!" Jet exclaimed.

Adan handed out the subs, and they stood around the kitchen island to eat.

"You told them not to take the pile by the door, right?"

Solana swallowed before answering. "Of course."

The movers had already cleared out the living room furniture. Now they took the dining chairs two at a time. Next, they loaded up the table and stacks of boxes before finishing with the guest bedroom furniture.

"Are you sure you don't want the furniture from the owner's suite?" Solana asked.

"Edward has someone coming by tomorrow to pick it up. A young couple from the church who have fallen on hard times."

"Alright. I put the rest of the food and beverages in the cooler by the door. There wasn't much left, but if we can get a bag of ice when we gas up the truck, then it won't go to waste."

Adan hugged Solana to his side, amazed at her foresight. Running a home came naturally to her. He'd miss that, especially once he and Jet settled in their own place. Adan dreaded figuring out how to cook for them. Maybe he could strike up a deal with Drake for some kind of meal plan for dinners from the dining hall.

"Let's load up. It looks like the movers are almost done," he said, tossing the sub wrappers in the trash.

Solana tied up the trash bag and carried it out while Jet helped him load suitcases, a few small boxes, the cooler, and computers in the truck. With one last look around the house, Adan felt confident they got everything.

The movers slid the ramp back into the truck and closed the door. After they drove away, Adan locked the house and met Solana and Jet in his truck.

"Let's pray before we head over to the Lazy D for the horses."

He laced his fingers with Solana's and bowed his head, grateful that she had softened toward him again. He prayed for safe travels for them and their household goods. Then he prayed God would bring the right family to the house in His timing. Solana prayed for him and Jet to find a new home and routine soon. Then all three of them echoed an "Amen."

With each mile of road behind him, Adan felt some of his grief lift, though a new heaviness settled in its place — the responsibility of being Jet's dad, mentor, and provider. He silently prayed for wisdom and discernment in his new role.

A few minutes later, he drove down the gravel drive of the Lazy D, angling the truck toward the horse trailer he'd dropped off six days ago. Solana hopped out of the passenger seat to guide him back.

"You're good!"

He cut the engine and secured the hitch. When Jet followed him around, observing the process, Adan realized it made a good teaching moment. So he explained the what and why behind each step.

Cooper Dunbar led Silver Streak toward them. After a friendly greeting, Adan showed Jet how to load the horses. Then he helped his son load Optimus, relieved that the horse didn't have an issue with trailers.

As they worked, he noticed Solana and Emeline chatting.

"Where you want the tack?" Cooper asked, drawing his attention away from the women.

"It's not rented?"

Cooper shook his head. "Nope. Annabel owned both saddles and more."

Adan crossed over to the storage door of the trailer. "Let's put it in here."

Once that was done, he called out to Lanni, eager to get on the road for the eight-hour drive home. It'd be dark by the time they made it back to Wickenburg. Then he'd have to drop the horses at Vargas Ranch. It was gonna be a long day, full of bittersweet goodbyes. Lanni being the hardest of them all.

"GOOD TO SEE you again, Emeline," Solana greeted her new friend. They exchanged contact info and Solana promised to give them updates about Jet.

"Annabel would have loved you," Emeline said. "You're a kind and caring soul. Perfect step-mom for Jet."

Heat crept up Solana's cheeks. The Dunbars seemed to believe she and Adan were a couple, but she didn't know how they got that impression and couldn't bring herself to tell them otherwise. Still, it felt good to hear someone thought she would be an excellent mother.

"Can I ask you something about Annabel and Arturo?"

"Sure."

"Why didn't she marry him?"

"Oh, she loved him with all her heart. Had the cancer not taken her life, they would have been a family. But the moment she learned about her diagnosis, she pushed him away. I'm uncertain why, but I think she didn't want him tied down with a kid that wasn't his own."

Emeline looked towards the mountains before continuing. "I suspect she prayed he would find a new love given time and could start a family without worrying about Jet."

"You think it'd be alright if we tried to explain that to Jet? He seemed upset saying goodbye to Arturo on Sunday."

Emeline patted her arm. "I think that's a great idea. He sure is gonna need your tender care in the coming weeks and months."

"Lanni! It's time to go."

Solana wrapped Emeline in a hug. "I'm so glad we met. Send me pictures of the little one when he arrives."

Emeline sighed and rested a hand on her baby bump. "Hoping she comes any day now."

As Solana started toward the truck, Emeline called after

her. "We'll be praying for all of you!"

She turned and waved at the kind couple. Maybe one day they could come back to visit.

Adan held the door for her and snuck a light kiss on her cheek as she settled into the passenger seat. He rounded the truck and drove away from the Lazy D.

Solana sighed and flipped down the vanity mirror to check on Jet. His thousand-yard stare out the window came as no surprise. He was leaving behind the last familiar thing in his life.

Lord, help him adjust to life with Adan. Help him learn to trust him and love him. Though she wanted to pray that she could become his step-mom, she stopped short. If she and Adan were destined to be together, then it would happen in God's timing. She certainly didn't want to rush it.

Okay, so maybe she did, but she wouldn't. She wanted God's plan for her life.

"We do not deviate from the Lord's plan," she whispered into the silent cab.

"Hmm. Good reminder for us all," Adan said as he laced his fingers with hers.

The trip home went much the same as the trip out. Solana turned on the satellite radio to a Christian station. She, Adan, and Jet played road-trip games. They stopped for fuel and bathroom breaks. The sun set around the time they left Flagstaff after a stop for dinner.

Even though she offered to drive, Adan declined. When Jet dozed in the back, her eyelids became heavy too.

Sometime later, Solana felt the truck slowing. She opened her eyes and stretched her arms.

"About another twenty minutes or so," Adan said.

"Thanks."

He cleared his throat. "I should thank you." He turned his hand over on the console, wiggling his fingers so Solana entwined hers with his. "I can't tell you how much it meant that you came with us. You helped in so many ways."

He lifted her hand, keeping his eyes on the road, and pressed his lips to it, his beard rough against her skin. Warmth spread from the contact up her arm and nestled in her heart. She would miss him so very much.

"When we get settled, I want to take you to dinner."

She angled toward him, blinking away her confusion.

"I owe you at least that much."

Her shoulders slumped. Of course, he wanted to take her to dinner as payment for her assistance. Not because he wanted to date her. She loosened her fingers from his and reached for the soda cup, feigning thirst.

Jet stirred in the backseat, ending their private moment.

"We'll talk more later," he whispered.

"'Kay."

Then he asked her to text his mama that they were almost home and had already eaten. She did so before turning the music up. She sang softly along with the lyrics of a song, reminding her that God worked all things together for the good of those who loved Him. The words became a prayer for Jet in her heart. She would miss taking care of him.

When Adan parked along the curb at his parents' house, they stood on the porch waiting for him to turn off the truck. Solana hopped out of the vehicle and, after a quick greeting, she helped them unload Adan and Jet's things. Then she tucked her suitcase and a box of books in the trunk of her Cherokee.

She entered the Franco's house and hugged Jet, biting the inside of her cheek to keep her tears from forming.

"I'll see you at church in a few days," she said as she tousled his hair.

"Bye, Solana. I'll miss you."

Well, there was no stopping the tears after that. She hurried out to her SUV, brushing the back of her hand over her damp cheeks.

"Hey, Lanni, wait up!"

Adan caught her right before she opened the door. He

turned her to face him. Then he caressed his thumb over her cheek before dropping a sweet kiss on her lips.

"I'll follow you back to the ranch." He jerked his head toward his truck. "Still gotta unload the horses."

"Oh. I could take them."

"Naw. Dylan's waiting to help me. We've got some catching up to do."

"Good night, Adan."

"Night, Lanni. See you soon."

She waved over her shoulder before sliding behind the wheel. Then she drove away from the Franco's, leaving a piece of her heart with Adan's son.

When Solana turned off the main highway and headed to the women's housing, Adan flashed his lights and took the opposite driveway toward the stables. Losing his presence felt as wide as the Grand Canyon. She loved Adan Franco deeper than she thought possible.

And she did not know where their relationship stood. Nor would she ask. He needed time to settle into his new responsibilities, find a house, and more. Even though they worked at the same ranch, she held no expectation of seeing him before church on Sunday. A fresh wave of tears rolled down her face at the thought.

14

ADAN EASED OUT of the cab of his truck, legs sore and stiff from the long drive. He leaned over and rubbed his knee. Exhaustion settled into his back. It'd be another few hours before he could crawl into his bed.

While he waited for Dylan, he reclined against the front fender of his truck. His phone pinged with a message from his friend saying he was headed to the stables. Then it chimed again. His dad finished bedtime prayers with Jet.

The sound of tires crunching on the gravel came from behind him. Then an engine silenced. Adan turned to see Dylan approach.

"Hey, Adan," Dylan said before giving him a hearty man hug. "I asked Ross to help so we can get you on the road sooner."

Adan's shoulders sank in relief. "Thanks, Dyl."

He shook out his legs as he walked to the back of the trailer. First out was Optimus Prime.

Dylan whistled. "He's a beauty."

"Optimus Prime, meet Dylan Vargas."

Dylan rubbed a hand down Optimus's face and neck. "Strong. He's what, five?"

"I think around that."

"Your son is fortunate to have such a fine horse at his age. Braden is gonna be jealous."

Adan snorted. "I doubt it. At least not when you give

him the one you've been shopping for."

Dylan sighed. "It's hard to find one trained for a double amputee."

"Get one young enough and you can train him."

Dylan led Optimus to the corral and opened the gate.

"Between Braden, Aubrey, and Brisa's morning sickness, I'm not sure I can take on much more."

"Wait, what? You knocked up my sister again?"

Dylan's face turned crimson and Adan laughed, nudging his shoulder.

"You know I'm teasing. When's the baby due?"

"Not sure. She has an appointment next week. I probably shouldn't have said anything. We haven't announced it yet."

"No worries. I won't tell Mama. But if she doesn't suspect it already, you'll need to tell her soon."

"We'll say something at the first family dinner after her appointment."

"Congrats."

Adan hugged Dylan again before turning toward the trailer to get Silver Streak.

"Ah, she is an oldy, huh?"

"She was Annabel's barrel racer back in our rodeo days. She's around nineteen."

"You know we'll take good care of her."

"The rancher who looked after her in New Mexico said she doesn't like male riders."

"Good to know. Wonder if she might be a good equine therapy horse."

"Dunno."

Adan closed the gate on the corral as Ross Braxton parked his truck near the stables. Ross greeted him.

"So, a kid?"

Adan bit back a growl. Guess the rumor mill had already been churning.

"Yup. My son's name is Jet."

Ross nodded before rubbing his hands together. "Let's get this trailer unhitched so you can head home."

Ross and Dylan made quick work of it. He said his farewells, promising to come back to work on Monday next week. That'd give him and Jet time to rest tomorrow. Then enroll Jet in school for Thursday. Then start house hunting.

As Adan drove down the gravel road out of the ranch, he came to the fork and slowed. He glanced at the clock on his dash. Ten at night. If he turned right, he'd be on his way home. If he veered left, he could see if Lanni was still awake and give her the goodnight kiss he should have earlier.

The clock blinked to one minute after ten and he made his choice. When he cut the engine, Solana emerged from the place she shared with her sister, wrapping a shawl around her.

Adan's heart raced as she met him by his truck.

"Forget something, cowboy?"

The bravery that had been his companion during bull riding competitions surfaced. He reached for her, drawing her to his chest. Then he lodged his hand in her hair and captured her lips with his, surprising them both. As she melted against him, he deepened the kiss, pressing her closer. She ran her hands up his arms until one rested behind his neck. The other raked through his hair, lighting a fierce fire within him. He loved her with every fiber of his being.

Common sense awoke, and he tore his lips from hers. Her chest rose and fell with ragged breaths, matching his own.

"Lanni." The rugged quality of his voice sounded foreign. Adan rested his chin on her shoulder and whispered in her ear. "I realized I forgot to kiss you goodnight."

Her sweet laughter floated on the cool breeze, causing joy to build in his chest. Before she could respond, he placed a finger over her swollen lips. Then he released her, pointing her toward the porch.

"Night, Lanni. Call you tomorrow?"

"Uh. Sure."

Oh, the tone of her voice, a mixture of surprise and reverence, made him want to drop to one knee. Except the timing was all wrong. They needed to talk, and a serious conversation would have to wait a few more days or weeks.

Adan smiled as he drove home. At least he didn't leave her guessing how he felt about her. Think that message came through loud and clear.

SOLANA BREATHED DEEPLY of the cool night air. Adan drove over just to give her a goodnight kiss. A smile broke across her face, and she jogged in place from the pure elation. She noticed the curtain falling back into place. Straightening her shoulders, she opened the door and stepped inside, draping the shawl over the back of a chair.

Renata stood in the open doorway of her room. "Did I just see that?"

Solana grinned. "Yes. He came back to kiss me goodnight." She sighed and stretched her arms out by her side before falling back onto the couch.

"Sounds like you two are dating."

"We haven't defined it yet. But, yeah, he's kissed me a few times."

"About time."

Solana sprang upright, her mood dampening. "Why do you say it like that?"

Renata rubbed her back. "It's just that you two have loved each other for years, but were both afraid to admit it. Everyone has seen it."

Her eyes rounded. "Everyone?"

"Everyone. Mom and Dad. Heidi and Harley. Most, if not all, of our cousins and their wives. Aunt Catalina. Tres. Even our grandfather saw it before he passed."

"That's two years ago. Why didn't you tell me before now?"

"You each had to work it out at your own pace."

Renata pushed away from the doorway to her room and crossed to the fridge. After pouring a glass of water, she turned toward Solana.

"Telling you… It would have only made you more frustrated. You could have pushed him too hard. Or done something you'd regret."

Solana straightened. "Rennie, are we still talking about me?"

Her sister's eyes glistened and darted away.

"What's wrong?"

Renata shook her head before she waved one hand in the air. "Its ancient history."

"The cowboy?"

"Yeah." Renata crossed the room and placed a hand on Solana's shoulder. "I'm happy for you and Adan. Trust God's timing in everything. Remember, He works everything out for good for those who love Him. He'll show you the way and the timing. Even when it doesn't feel like He's working, He is."

Renata leaned down and hugged Solana. Solana patted her sister's back.

"Love you, Rennie."

"I love you, too. Sweet dreams, little sister."

Then Renata went to bed, closing the door behind her.

Solana turned off the lights in the main part of their apartment before she turned in.

Rennie was right about so many things. She would have tried to force a confession from Adan long before now if she had realized he loved her. By being oblivious, it benefited her. His kiss tonight had been real. Honest. An accurate reflection of his heart. She would never doubt it.

THE NEXT MORNING, Solana hurried through her routine, unpacking her suitcase from the trip as she went. As she entered the kitchen, she started a pot of coffee, missing Adan and Jet already. It was only the first morning without them.

Her thumb hovered over the ongoing messages with Adan. While the rich aroma of brewing coffee filled the air, she typed out a text. Then deleted it before starting a new one. By her third attempt, the coffee sputtered to a stop. She poured a mug and reread the message. Yeah, she could send that.

Praying you and Jet have a great day.

She wanted to ask what his plans were. She wanted to tag along.

A deep sigh burst through the silence. She sat down on a bar stool at the island and opened her Bible study app. The words of Psalm 86:5-7 filled her heart and soul. "For you, Lord, are kind and ready to forgive, abounding in faithful love to all who call on you. Lord, hear my prayer; listen to my cries for mercy. I call on you in the day of my distress, for you will answer me."

Lord, let this be my prayer. And Adan's and Jet's. Let us call on You in the days of our distress. Surround them both with Your comfort. Thank you for forgiving me for my impatience and self- ishness. You are so faithful.

Solana continued to read. Verses 11-12 practically leaped from the page. "Teach me your way, Lord, and I will live by your truth. Give me an undivided mind to fear your name. I will praise you with all my heart, Lord my God, and will honor your name forever."

Yes, Lord. Teach me Your way. I want to live by your truth. I want You to be the center of my life — not Adan or Jet. No matter how much I love them, I want to love You more. I want to honor your name forever. Show me Your ways. Amen.

As she opened her eyes, joy rose in her soul. She sang words of praise to God from one worship song as she re-filled the travel mug. Then she left, locking the door behind her. She continued singing in the privacy of her car as she drove over to the dining hall. When the last refrain left her lips, she smiled and shut off her car.

God had been so very good to her. And Adan. And Jet. A peace settled in her heart as she prayed silently for Jet. God would continue to be faithful to the boy who lost every-thing. Solana knew it without a doubt.

15

_____

DROPPED JET OFF at school. Check. Unpacked the rest of Jet's clothes. Check. Groceries ordered for pick up. Check. Laundry started. Check.

"I would have done that for you," Mama said as Adan closed the washer with a satisfied smile, the scent of fresh fabric softener lingering in the air.

"Mama, I appreciate you letting us stay here, but I don't expect maid services."

She smiled. "Well, if you want to take off for your house hunting appointments, I can transfer this load and fold it."

Adan's neck muscles loosened. It would be nice to have the help. Before picking Jet up from school, he had a jam-packed schedule. And he hadn't talked to or seen Solana since they came back from Albuquerque. They'd only texted once.

"Yeah, thanks Mama. That'd be a big help."

Adan glanced at his watch. He could drive over to the ranch and pick up Solana. He'd love to see her and hear her thoughts on the houses. Yeah, that's what he'd do.

His thumbs blazed across his phone. *Can I kidnap you for the afternoon?*

Solana: *Hmm… One sec.*

Adan sure hoped they weren't too busy.

Solana: *Renata says you owe her. I'll be ready when you get here. See you soon.*

His heart warmed when she signed off with kissy lips and hearts. Good. She wasn't too mad about him practically ghosting her.

He whistled as he grabbed his keys and left. After he parked near the office half an hour later, Solana appeared before he could turn off the truck. About to leave the truck running to get the door, she waved him off. She opened the passenger door, and instantly the scent of her filled the cab, soothing his anxiety. Once she settled in the seat, he leaned over and dropped a kiss on her lips. Mmm. He'd been waiting three long days to do that. Her cheeks turned pink while he backed out.

"So, what's our mission, stranger?"

"Guess I deserve that."

She nudged his arm. "I know you have a ton on your plate. I'm not upset."

"Thanks for understanding." He threaded his fingers with hers as their hands rested on the center console.

"We house hunting?"

"Yeah. The first couple of places are in Forepaugh. I'd love to be close to the ranch. But that means we'll be far from Jet's school."

"Jet's gonna be driving in a few years, so that won't be bad."

Adan coughed and pounded a fist against his chest as he turned onto the road, headed to Forepaugh. "Let's not rush things. I only found out about him two weeks ago."

Solana chuckled. "He's twelve going on thirteen. Him driving will come sooner than you think."

He twisted his lips, scrunched his nose, and frowned.

"And he'll start dating, too."

"Are you trying to give me a heart attack? If so, I name you his guardian, should anything happen to me."

"I'd love to take care of Jet."

Her softening voice thrilled him. Maybe she wouldn't mind becoming Jet's step-mom. The idea brought him more comfort than he expected. Then thoughts of little dark-haired kids running around a big house caused his cheeks to heat. Thank goodness his beard hid the worst of it.

"We're here."

"Hey, isn't that Brisa's rental just down the street?"

"Yeah."

A memory crossed his mind from when he and Dylan organized the remodeling of that house. Right after his sister moved home with her double amputee son, Braden. Adan instantly connected with his nephew. Though Brisa never told him about the darkest parts of her past, he suspected she'd suffered a lot. Adan found out about Dylan's long-held feelings for Brisa after they remodeled her house to be wheelchair accessible.

He sighed. Seemed like a long time ago. Had it been five years already?

On that day, he and Solana remodeled the owner's bathroom together. His lips curved into a slight smile. What a fool he'd been when she strode across the lawn and demanded to work with him. He tousled her hair, as if she were a little girl. She must have been about twenty back then. Definitely a woman.

That day changed his perception of her. He *had* noticed everything about her. Her perfect figure and fun personality. Her servant's heart. She worked as hard as him in that bathroom. They removed all the tile, then reshaped the entrance to the shower into a gently sloped ramp so Braden could wheel into it. The next day they re-tiled it.

As they worked together, they developed a friendship. Easy banter mixed with a touch of flirting. Adan had almost mixed the grout wrong. She playfully called him the pretty one, suggesting he let the brains of the operation — her — read the instructions. That day marked the start of their ongoing joke, pitting her as the smart one against him as the pretty one. Even back then, he thought she lived up to both monikers.

"What's that smirk for?" Lanni asked as she opened the truck door.

Adan shook his head. "Just remembering the bathroom remodel."

She tossed her head back and laughed. "I almost decked you when you rubbed your knuckles on my head like I was twelve."

"I deserved it," he admitted as he joined her at the front door.

He check his phone for the code from the realtor, then he punched it on the keypad. He would meet up with the realtor after the first two.

"I was so frustrated that you treated me like a kid that day."

Adan expelled a loud breath as he clasped her hand. "Yeah, I was pretty dense." He leaned forward and pecked her cheek. "Sorry I wasted so much time."

Solana winked at him. "Shall we check out this place?"

He handed her his phone so she could read the details about the house.

"Only sixteen hundred square feet?"

"Yeah. Seems a little small if we want more kids." The words flew out of his mouth before he thought better of them.

"Adan Franco. You ghost me for several days and now you have me popping out kids? I think you're missing a few steps in this relationship."

His face and neck heated hotter than a mid-summer day at the ranch. Then he winked at her. "You're not wrong."

"Do we need to see more? It's definitely not big enough for a growing family."

"Guess not. What's next?" he asked, since she still held his phone.

"This one sounds better. Twenty-four hundred square feet. Four bedrooms, great room, and a separate playroom."

"Alright, navigate away."

A few minutes later, they parked in front of the house. He liked the curb appeal. Touring the house, Solana shared her preferences and asked for his. Adan's heart knotted. Sure felt like they were a couple looking for their first home together. Any doubt he had about sharing the rest of his life with her faded away. He wanted Lanni as his wife.

Maybe he should propose to her before buying a house. Before getting settled with his son. It would be perfect, marrying her soon so the three of them could move into the house together. But was it what she wanted?

He had missed her so much this week. Even Jet mentioned her at least once a day, wondering when she'd come over. Their time in Albuquerque bonded them together as a family. It was what he wanted more than anything.

Yet, they had only just taken the first few tentative steps into an undefined relationship. Moving from years-long friends to a romantic relationship.

As he held the truck door open for her, all the words he wanted to say jammed up behind a dozen warning bells not to rush in. He needed to pray about it before making a move.

SOLANA FLUNG THE truck door open at the third house, battling giddiness and annoyance. Adan's comment about kids at the first house threw her into an inner emotional tug of war. She had waited years for him to notice her. Now he'd made the mental leap from a few kisses to marriage, kids, and a home together. Even if it was her heart's truest desire, she wasn't sure she wanted to rush things that fast.

As they stepped into the kitchen of the thirty-six hundred square foot, five-bedroom, three and a half bath house, her jaw dropped. A chef's fridge gleamed against the pristine white cabinets. Light quartz counters sparkled as their length rivaled Aunt Catalina's home. Double ovens on one side. A six burner gas cooktop. This was a cook's dream kitchen—her dream kitchen. She ran her hand along the cold, smooth countertop as she walked toward the massive pantry.

Something along the hall near the pantry caught her eye. "A butler's pantry? Adan! I've always wanted—" She pursed her lips tight. This would not be her home.

The realtor glanced over at them from the other end of the great room. Solana's face burned. She should not act like she had a say in buying the house. Their relationship may never progress to something more. Adan was a single dad now. No matter his dreaming earlier, he needed to get used to life with a preteen son first. Right?

Adan slipped an arm around her waist as he examined the butler's pantry. "Hmm. But we don't have a butler."

We. There was that hint of something more.

She swatted at his arm playfully. "No butler required. It is a nice place to pre-stage things for a holiday meal or it could be a spot for Jet's after-school snacks."

He shrugged. Then he whispered close to her ear, his warm breath sending ripples of awareness down her arms. "What do you say we check out the owner's suite?"

She closed her eyes as he wrapped his arms around her.

"Hmm. This might be a cozy spot for sneaking kisses." Then he pressed his lips against her neck. "Yeah, I think you've sold me on the kissing nook."

"Adan!"

He whirled away, clasping her hand before leading her to the owner's suite. Solana's eyes bulged as he opened the door.

"Oh, my."

"It's huge. Bigger than three bedrooms at my parents' house," Adan said. "What would we… I do with all this space?"

Solana fell in love with the room. The vast windows provided a stunning view of the always-green luxury fake grass overlooking the valley with Dalton Peak in the background. She pictured a chaise lounge tucked at an angle in the corner next to a reading lamp and a small table. A pleasant retreat from a day of chasing kids around. The room had plenty of space for dressers, a king bed, end tables, and more.

"Check out this closet," Adan said from somewhere deep in the bathroom section of the suite.

She loved the fixtures in the beautifully appointed bathroom. A soaker tub. Split sinks. This home was turning into her dream home. And it sat at the end of a private driveway perched on the side of the next mountain over from Dalton Peak. Close to work and family. Not any further from Wickenburg than she lived now.

As Solana continued through the owner's bathroom, she found Adan in a massive closet. The L-shaped room rivaled the size of her room back on the ranch. Except it was just for clothes and shoes! She spread out her arms and spun in a circle.

"Looks like you'll need to buy more clothes," she teased him.

"Ha. You like it?"

She stopped abruptly, whirling to face him. "Adan—"

"Lanni, do you like it?"

Her voice faded to a whisper. "I love it. The entire house."

"Then I'm gonna buy it."

"But—"

His phone rang, and he glanced at it.

"Uh, oh. It's Jet's school. Can you tell the realtor I want to put in an offer?"

Solana left him standing there as he answered the call. She found the realtor in the great room.

"He wants to put in an offer on it."

The realtor quirked a brow. "What about you?"

"Oh, we're not… We're just dating. It's for him and his

son."

If her words surprised the realtor, she did a great job of hiding her reaction. "I will get the paperwork started."

"We need to go," Adan said as he stepped into the room. "Jet got into a fight at school."

Solana's heart squeezed tight. "Is he alright?"

"Yeah. He's in the principal's office. I have to pick him up early."

"You want me to come? I can call to see if someone can take me back home?"

"I can drop you at Vargas Ranch," the realtor volunteered. "Adan, can you call me as you drive and we can talk about what you want to offer?"

"Sure thing. Thanks for taking Lanni home."

Adan dropped a kiss on Solana's cheek before he hurried out the door.

"I'll call later," she said before the door on the perfect house closed.

"Shall we go?" the realtor asked.

Solana nodded as she followed the woman to her SUV, praying for Jet and Adan on the short drive home. She could hardly believe Jet would have started a fight. Not being there for him caused a deep ache in the pit of her stomach, reminding her it wasn't her place.

16

—————

BY THE TIME Adan arrived at Jet's school, he had worked out the offer details with the realtor. He parked his truck in the visitor spot and headed toward the office. It seemed a little surreal to enter the principal's office at a school he had once attended.

"Adan! Nice to see you."

Adan's jaw slackened. The principal was none other than Marcus Horne, a former classmate. "You're the principal?"

Marcus chuckled. "For five years running."

Adan extended a hand, and Marcus shook it, a brief but firm grip, then indicated a seat with a subtle nod. With a weary sigh, Adan eased into the hard chair, the wooden legs creaking under his weight as he shook his head slowly.

"Guess you went into education."

"Yeah. After a brief attempt at bronco riding, teaching seemed safer." Marcus smoothed his hands over the top of his desk. "Sorry to drag you down here early, but Jet threw a punch at another kid."

"What happened?"

"Seems the kid mouthed off about barrel racers."

Disappointment settled over Adan, a heavy cloak that made him press his lips together in a thin line.

"Jet got upset and took the first swing."

"I'm sorry about that. I only took guardianship of him

two weeks ago. His late mother was a barrel racer. She died from a long battle with cancer and I've uprooted him from his home on top of it."

Marcus shook his head. "Can't have been easy for him. Listen, given the circumstances and that Jet is still adjusting, I'll let it slide this time. But, if he gets in a fight again, he'll face a suspension. We try to nip fighting in the bud. The other kid is on a three-day suspension."

"Understood. Where's my son?"

Marcus pressed a button on his desk phone and asked the secretary to send Jet in.

A purplish-red, swollen welt marred the skin around Jet's eye and cheekbone. A wave of protectiveness washed over Adan, every instinct flaring as he schooled his features. He stood, fists clenched at his sides, the silence amplifying the pounding of his heart. Taking a slow breath, he prayed for the words to say.

Crouching to eye level with Jet, he asked, "What happened?"

Tears shimmered in Jet's eyes, his face contorting as he struggled to speak. "He was saying bad stuff about my mama."

"Did he use her name?"

Jet shook his head before he wiped his nose on the sleeve of his shirt.

"So he wasn't saying something about your mama?"

"He said barrel racers were buckle bunnies. Said they were looking for a man to father their kids so they could get rich."

Adan inwardly cringed, struggling with how accurate the kid's description could have been for some women who hung around the rodeo. Not about barrel racers, though. And certainly not Annabel.

"What happened next?"

"I told him my mama wasn't like that and I told him to shut up. When he didn't, I punched him."

Adan sucked in a long breath as his foot grew numb. Maybe he should have stayed seated in the rickety chair. "I'm sorry he said mean things that aren't true about barrel racers. But punching him was just as wrong."

Jet's chin jutted into the air, his arms crossed tightly over his chest, a silent challenge in his stance. Seeing his son's defiant posture, a surge of resolve filled Adan, making him determined to use this as a teaching moment.

"Apologize to Principal Horne for trying to settle your dispute the wrong way."

"But what Tyler said was wrong."

"That may be true. However, a wrong action in exchange for wrong words only leads to trouble. You were just as much to blame as Tyler. Now, apologize."

"I'm sorry."

Adan stood to his full height, placing a hand on Jet's shoulder. Then he turned toward Marcus. "If it wouldn't be too much trouble, I'd like Tyler's parents' phone number so Jet can apologize to Tyler this evening."

"Unfortunately, because of privacy concerns, I can't give out their information. If you'd like to contact them through the parents' portal, you may."

Adan thought he had the info about the website in an email they sent him after registering Jet. He would look it up later. It was important to help the boys clear the air so things didn't get out of control again.

"Alright. Thanks for your help, Principal Horne."

Marcus shook his hand before Adan walked Jet to the truck.

He drove them home in silence. Once inside, he sent Jet to his room and told him they would talk more later.

Adan's phone pinged with the reminder to pick up his grocery order. After updating his mama about Jet, he went to get his groceries before coming back.

The day wore on as he saw to several other errands and chores. It wasn't until after dinner he sat down to talk to Jet, still uncertain about the best way to handle things.

He knocked on Jet's bedroom door, hesitant yet determined to face whatever awaited him inside. As the door creaked open, Jet wore the same scowl from earlier. The tension between them hung heavy in the air, unspoken words and unresolved issues lurking beneath the surface.

Adan prayed silently for the words. Something his dad used to say came to mind. Maybe that would help his own son.

"Tell me what you're feeling," Adan said as he perched on the edge of the bed.

Jet unfolded his arms. His lip quivered and his eyes darted away. "I miss my mama."

"Go on."

"Was my mama was like Tyler said? Did she want your money? Is that why you never came to see me?"

The question seared clean through his soul. "It was nothing like what Tyler said." Adan swallowed away a dozen lies that formed on his tongue. Opposing thoughts twisted his gut. He wanted to be honest with Jet. Yet, he must keep the secret about his son's birth father.

"Your mama and I were good friends. She was a barrel racer at many of the events where I competed as a bull rider. We laughed a lot. Talked about serious things sometimes, too."

He ran a hand through his hair. "As much as I would have loved to know you sooner, like I said before, your mama never told me about you. If she had, I would have been involved in your life from the beginning. I'm sorry for the years we lost. But we can't get them back, and I need you to trust that I love you and want the best for you."

Jet picked at his shirt's hem, seeming to consider the words.

With a sigh, Adan rubbed a hand down his face and beard, the rough texture a familiar comfort as he carefully proceeded. "There are some women like what Tyler said—

who try to manipulate a man's feelings and desires to take money from them. But there are also many honest women, like your mama, who earned their living competing or working at the rodeo. They loved their jobs and their sport."

He reached over and rested his hand on Jet's arm. "Your mama was decent, honest, and hardworking. She loved barrel racing. So did Silver Streak. They were an impressive pair. Won many awards. She also cared about the people around her. She became close friends with Zack's mama, Chrissy. I can't tell you how many times I saw her praying with someone or lending a shoulder to cry on."

"So, you see, even though Tyler was partly right, he was wrong about your mama and me. But even if he had been right, it was wrong to let your anger control you to the point of hurting someone else."

Jet sniffed. "I know. Mama would have been mad."

"Yeah. I'm disappointed 'cause I know you can do better." He swallowed down his own surprise. Sounded exactly like something Dad would have said.

"There are a couple of things I want you to think about. First, you've been through a lot and I'm sure there're all kinds of emotions boiling inside of you. It's important to let 'em out constructively. I like to talk with friends or God or write stuff down. You know you can talk to me."

"What about Solana? Can I talk to her?"

It thrilled Adan that Jet trusted Lanni. "Sure thing. We can call her later."

Jet straightened, and some of the harsh edges softened on his expression.

"Second, sometimes when kids are saying mean things, they don't know what they are talking about. People lie and generalize. We can't lash out every time someone does. Some kids will keep at you until you react. The best thing to do is ignore them. The Bible says that a fool does not delight in understanding but only wants to show off his opinions. That's what Tyler did today. Make sense?"

Jet's face lit and he nodded. "Yeah."

"So, what are you gonna do next week if Tyler runs his mouth?"

"Not punch him. And ignore him?"

"That's a good idea. You can also walk away or tell a teacher."

"Adan, can we call Solana now?"

"Sure, bud." He slid his phone from his shirt pocket, scrolling through his contacts. Then he pressed his thumb on her name. It barely rang when she answered.

"Did you get it?" She asked as she adjusted the phone so her face filled the frame.

"What?" Adan asked, uncertain what she was talking about.

"The house!" She shook her head and *tsked*. "Guess I *am* the smart one."

"Dunno yet."

"I heard from Emeline Dunbar. She delivered a healthy baby girl named Anna after Jet's mom."

"Send pictures and I'll share them with Jet."

"Sure thing." Solana paused. "Well, judging by the frilly pink curtains in the background, I'm guessing you're in Brisa's old room?"

Adan chuckled as he studied her gorgeous face. Yeah, letting Jet talk to her would be good. She just seemed to have a way with him. "Yup. Jet wants to talk to you."

Her eyes rounded. "Really?"

Adan nodded. "Here he is." To Jet he said, "When you're done, I want to talk to her."

Then he stood and headed to his room to check his email on his computer, trying not to eavesdrop on Jet's conversation with Solana through their thin walls. His heart nearly burst as he thought about how wonderful it would be to become a family.

Maybe it was time to buy a ring.

AS SOON AS Adan mentioned Jet wanted to speak with her, Solana quickly retreated to her bedroom. Disbelief washed over her; her heart pounded, struggling to reconcile that the preteen trusted her. She quickly settled into the fluffy comforter of her bed before gently asking Jet how he was doing, her voice soft with concern.

"I got into a fight today."

"So I heard. What happened?"

Jet's words painted a vivid picture, making her protectiveness boil over. She could barely contain the urge to confront Tyler. With a visible effort, she smoothed her features, determined to set a good example for Adan's son despite her inner turmoil.

Jet told her everything Adan said, leaving her stunned. For a man who just found out he had a son, Adan knew what he was doing. She could only hope to take to parenting as well as he did.

When Jet's expression clouded and his chin trembled, Solana asked him what was wrong.

"I miss my mama."

"Oh, Jet." Her arms ached with the desire to hold him, to whisper words of comfort. "Of course you do. And that's okay."

He swiped his shirtsleeve over his cheek. "I'm afraid I will forget her."

She blinked rapidly, feeling the full weight of his heartache. "We won't let that happen. I'm sure once you move into the new house, your dad will find a good place for pictures of her. And we can think about how to display her barrel racing awards. Maybe create something with pictures of her racing for the backdrop. How's that sound?"

"I'd like that. Will you help?"

"Of course. I'd love to."

"Lanni?"

She smiled at his use of her nickname. "Yeah?"

"Thanks."

Then the screen went blurry, showing the hallway wall in a jerky motion before Adan's face appeared again with his childhood bedroom wall in the background.

Solana expelled a loud breath and wiped a finger under each eye.

"Everything okay?"

She nodded. "Yeah. I love your son, you know. He's a good kid."

Adan's lips quirked in a half-smile. "You say that on the day he got into a fight."

"I know, but he is. His heart is pure. He's just working through his grief and trying to adjust to this strange new life." She glanced away from the screen. "I wish I could be there to hug him and tuck him in tonight."

Adan's features softened. "I think he would like that."

She cleared her throat, love and protectiveness filling her soul. "He's afraid he will forget her."

"No. We won't let that happen."

"That's along the same lines as what I said."

"I'll start jotting down memories from when I knew her. And when we get settled, we'll put up pictures of her."

Solana snorted. "Maybe you're smarter than I thought. That's what I said."

The conversation paused as she studied his face. Dark circles under his eyes hinted at the weight on his shoulders. She longed to curl up next to him and rub the stress from his neck or kiss away some of his worry. Every hour, every minute apart from her guys chipped away at her heart. She craved their presence as desperately as she craved the air filling her lungs.

"Oh, I just got a text from the realtor."

"And?"

He squinted and his lips moved silently for a few seconds before his face lit up brighter than the sunrise. "We got it!"

Excitement bubbled over. "You did? The one with the butler's pantry?"

"The kissing nook?" He waggled his eyebrows. "Yeah, we did."

Her heart pounded against her ribs as her face heated. Why did he keep saying 'we'? Did he mean him and Jet, or was she a part of the 'we' he had in mind? Was it possible Adan might want a lifetime together?

"She says we can close by the end of next week, since it's vacant."

A twinge of envy niggled deep in her heart. "That's wonderful. You and Jet will get into a routine soon."

A frown flashed across features. "Lanni, about—"

The sound of a knock on her door drew her attention. "One sec, Adan."

Rennie stuck her head in. "Hey, I'm not feeling well and a guest just texted they want to check in."

"At nine thirty at night?" Her shoulders sank. "Okay. Text them I'm on my way."

"Adan, I have to go. Love you."

Solana hung up before he could reply, scrambling to the edge of her bed. Then she donned a light jacket.

"You need anything?" she asked her sister.

"No. I'm gonna head to bed. Thanks for taking care of this."

"Anytime."

Solana left and drove over to the office. She greeted the couple as she unlocked the office.

"Any trouble finding us?"

"Nope. The directions on your website were perfect," the man answered.

Solana continued the conversation while she waited for her computer to wake up. Then she looked up their reservation, found their room, and ran the key cards through the coding machine. After she gave them directions to their room, she handed them a flier with the details about the breakfast buffet. She jotted her number in the corner, asking them to text or call if they needed anything tonight.

"Enjoy your stay." She waved as they pulled out of the parking lot. Then she locked up the office and drove home.

As she lay in bed, consumed by thoughts of Adan, a wave of restlessness washed over her. The weight of uncertainty settled upon her like a heavy blanket, making it hard to breathe. Adan's unfinished words gnawed at her, leaving her stomach tied in knots.

Did he love her? Did he want her as his wife and Jet's step-mom? When would they find time to talk about them and where they were headed as a couple? How much longer would she have to wait to find out?

The limbo state of their relationship caused sleep to elude her. Her thoughts spun in endless circles, stealing away the peace she so desperately craved. It was as if her entire being had become a battleground, where emotions clashed and vied for dominance.

At last, her eyes grew heavy, burdened by the weight of unanswered questions and Adan's unspoken words. The emotional rollercoaster had taken its toll, leaving her physically and emotionally depleted.

17

_____

ON SUNDAY MORNING, Adan rested a hand on Jet's shoulder at the back of the church. They had arrived early, anticipating some introductions. Now Adan second guessed that choice. Jet practically velcroed himself to Adan's side after meeting Catalina and Tres Vargas. Of course, Catalina invited them to Sunday supper after church. He gave a vague answer just in case Jet seemed even more uncomfortable.

"Morning."

Solana's greeting and bright smile eased some of his tension. He leaned down and pressed his lips to her cheek.

"Morning. You look amazing." And there was that pink hue coloring her cheeks. Something about it made him content.

"Jet, how are you?"

He shrugged one shoulder.

"Most of the Junior High and High School students attend the main service. Let me introduce you to my cousins' older kids."

Adan greeted Dylan and Brisa while Solana whisked Jet away to meet Felipa, who was only one year older than Jet. His nephew Braden tugged on his hand.

"Who's that?"

"That's my son, Jet."

Braden cocked his head to the side. "Does that make him

my cousin?"

Adan tousled his hair. "That it does."

Braden darted toward Solana, Jet, and Felipa, as sure-footed as ever on his artificial legs.

Brisa winked at Adan. His stomach tightened as he braced for questions—possibly about Jet. Maybe about Solana.

"So... Solana went with you, huh?"

Heat warmed Adan's face and neck. "She was a huge help. Very organized. And she's a skilled cook, too."

"I saw you greet her. 'Bout time the two of you started dating."

Dylan chuckled. "Adan, you two have liked each other for years. Brisa kept bugging me about saying something to you."

"Yeah, big brother. You're a little dense sometimes."

Adan rolled his eyes. "I think service is about to start."

Brisa laughed as he headed for their usual row. When Solana sat next to him, he laced his fingers with hers. Brisa was right. He'd been thickheaded concerning Lanni. Wasted so many years they could have been together all because of unfounded fears. Although he wished things were different, all he could do was move forward.

As the service started, Jet seemed to relax. So did Adan. It felt good to be worshipping at his home church, with Lanni on one side and Jet on the other. Maybe life would settle into normal rhythms soon.

When the service finished, Adan offered Lanni a lift over to the Vargas ranch house for Sunday supper.

"Adan, can we go for a horse ride with Felipa and Braden?" Jet asked from the backseat.

"Let's see after the meal."

"Braden said his dad bought him a special saddle that he can use even when he doesn't wear his legs."

Adan held back a chuckle, finding Jet's way of describing Braden's disability accurate, even if it might sound odd to those who didn't know his nephew.

As soon as they arrived at the ranch house, Jet scurried inside.

"Guess he's eager to see his newly discovered cousin."

Lanni giggled. "Seems he and Braden have a few things in common—horses. And dads who work with horses."

Adan grasped her hand and kept hold of it inside the house, despite a few raised eyebrows from friends and family. She remained by his side until it was time to serve the meal. His sister deposited his niece Aubrey in his arms.

"Unca. Down."

Adan smiled at Aubrey's two-year-old pronunciation of "uncle."

"No Breezy. It's almost time for supper. Let's wash your hands."

"'Kay." Her green eyes rounded as she patted her hands together.

He carried her to the bathroom and helped her wash up. Then he propped her on a hip. When he entered the massive great room, his gaze collided with Solana's. She held Marlaine, Dalton and River's sixteen-month-old. Lanni looked perfectly at ease, holding a baby in one arm and a sippy cup in her other hand. The picture wrapped around his heart, increasing his longing for something more with her. She deposited Marlaine in a high chair. Aubrey and Derin's son, Maverick, used booster seats and still needed adult supervision.

Adan buckled Aubrey into her booster as the family gathered for the prayer. Jet stood next to his new friends, Braden and Felipa. Dalton's four-year-old twins stood next to Felipa around the kids' table. In a few more months, Aubrey and Maverick would join them.

Everyone finished the prayer together with the family motto: "We do not deviate from the Lord's plan."

His gut pinched, wondering if he had delayed the Lord's plan for him and Solana. Before he could dwell on the thought, Brisa got everyone's attention. Dylan wrapped his arm around her.

"We have some exciting news," she said.

"We're going to have another baby," Dylan said.

Loud chatter erupted, full of congratulations.

"When are you due?" Mama asked.

"Around June."

"Ay!" Catalina Vargas exclaimed. "Madison's due in March. Rennie in April. You in June."

"Don't forget Candi in April, too," Travis Kaine, Candi's dad, said.

Adan held Lanni's chair for her, biting back a teasing comment about needing to catch up. He must propose first and he still hadn't figured out the right time.

Once he settled, Lanni leaned over. "Guess Drake and Candi made that announcement while we were in New Mexico. I can't believe Rennie forgot to tell me."

During the meal, Adan treasured having Lanni at his side. It felt both new and normal. Love for her bubbled inside him. He glanced at her.

"What? Do I have lettuce in my teeth?"

Adan chuckled at her snarky remark. "You look perfect. I love you."

She pressed her shoulder against his arm. "I love you, too."

"Dad! Can we go on a horse ride now?" Braden hollered from the kids' table.

"We have to help clean up first," Dylan replied.

"We have plenty of help," Brisa said. "Why don't you take the older kids?"

"I'll come with," Adan volunteered, eager to catch up with Dylan and to watch Jet with his beloved horse.

"You ready?"

Jet nodded emphatically, eyes filled with glee.

Lanni snorted, but Adan dipped his head to plant a loud kiss on her lips, stopping whatever teasing she had in mind.

Instead, her face turned red.

"See you later." Then he winked at her before following Dylan, Braden, Felipa, and Jet to Dylan's vehicle.

"That's new," he said. "Mini van?"

"Brisa wanted to upgrade. Said a family of five sorta needs it. Plus, we've removed the second middle bucket seat so we can lock in Braden's wheelchair."

Felipa and Jet scooted into the third row while Braden climbed into his wheelchair. Guess they left it there even when he wore his prosthetics.

After they arrived at the stables, Jet and Felipa groomed their horses. Dylan helped Braden with his. Adan spent a few minutes with Silver Streak, sneaking her a special treat. She seemed to warm up to him. After one last pat, he retrieved Trixie Wind.

"Felipa, can you stay with Braden while I get my horse?" Dylan asked.

Even though she agreed, Adan waited to mount Trixie Wind, watching all three kids. As soon as Dylan emerged from the stables, Braden led them, chattering the entire way. Felipa rode on one side of him, Jet on the other. Adan positioned his horse behind the kids so he could talk with Dylan.

"Congrats, Dyl. Guess Bri was further along than you thought."

"Yeah. Caught us by surprise."

"Hoping for a boy or girl?"

Dylan chuckled. "I'll take anything as long as there are no twins."

"Careful, that doesn't rule out triplets."

Dylan scowled at him for a few seconds before changing the subject. "You and Solana are finally official?"

"A couple? Yes."

"Engaged?"

"Soon."

A grin stretched across his friend's face. "Good. It's been clear to most everyone who knows you that you're a perfect pair. What took you so long?"

Adan let out a long breath. "I know. I waited much longer than I should have. I spent too many years trying to convince myself I was too old for her. Or she was too young for me. Now, after losing Jet's mother, I realize how fleeting life is. She was my age, Dyl."

"I'll admit, hearing you had a son surprised me. I know you mentioned not keeping it pure during a few years in the rodeo."

"Honestly, it was one year."

"I thought…"

"Spit it out, Dyl."

"I'm having a hard time wrapping my head around you not being a part of Jet's life before now. It's not like you."

Adan slowed Trixie, creating more space between them and the kids, yet still close enough they could react to any danger.

"His mama never told me about him. She barely told me she was leaving the rodeo. Never knew why. Her only explanation back then had been that it was time."

"You never suspected?"

Adan's stomach knotted. He'd never kept a secret from Dylan before. Yet, he felt Annabel would not appreciate him telling anyone. To his family and friends—everyone except Lanni—he must maintain the ruse.

"Never suspected anything. We lost touch after she left."

"Well, I'm glad you get to raise him now. If you're as good of a dad as you are an uncle, you'll do alright."

"Just alright?"

Dylan reached over and patted his shoulder. "Yeah. Brisa wouldn't forgive me if I let you think otherwise."

Adan chuckled before kicking Trixie Wind to a trot. Riding next to his son, his heart filled to overflowing. Even if they shared no DNA, Jet had become the son of his heart. He felt honored to finish what Annabel started—caring for a young man in the making.

SOLANA HAD BEEN avoiding her parents during the meal, fearing they might judge her. As soon as Adan vacated the chair next to her, Mom slid into it.

"Are you and Adan dating?"

"Yes."

"Finally!"

That was not the reaction she expected, especially after Dad's stern warning before the road trip. "Come again?"

"I'm happy for you, Lanni. I know you've wanted something to spark and grow. Your dad and I have been praying that God's plan for your life would become clear. And I think it's starting to take shape, don't you?"

Slowly, Solana nodded. The image of Adan holding his niece flashed across her mind. Every single time she saw him hold a child, it pulled on her heartstrings, making the longing for a life with him even stronger. He was a great dad and uncle.

"Be patient," Mom warned. "He clearly loves you, but don't rush him into any decisions about your relationship. Be content in the present."

Solana's shoulders sagged. Patience had never been easy for her.

"God's plan, Lanni. Not yours. Not mine."

"I know. I'll try to be patient."

"And remember, he's still adjusting to being a dad. Did I hear Heidi say he bought a house?"

"Yeah, they're gonna close on it next week. Move in as soon as possible after."

Mom patted her hand. "See, that's a lot of change."

"Agreed."

"Now, let's get this table cleared so we can grill Brisa about being eight-weeks along before telling us."

Solana giggled, a little relieved to have the attention divert from her.

As she and her cousins-in-law cleared the table, Marlaine cried. Soon Maverick joined in. Derin scooped up his son, whispering comforting sounds. She shook her head, still getting used to seeing him as a dad. Now they had a second one on the way. Dalton lifted Marlaine from her booster, smoothing her hair out of her eyes.

"What's wrong Marley girl?"

She pouted and jammed her thumb into her mouth, mumbling something.

"No, you can't have ice cream. Abuela baked churros for later."

Solana smiled as she headed back into the dining room to clear several serving dishes. The smoky aroma of pork carnitas still hung heavy in the air, a scent she associated with many homey, comforting memories. The sound of a football game echoed through the great room. Men's voices added to the noise. When she stepped into the kitchen, the women were carrying on at least two different conversations. A peace wrapped around her soul. She loved this loud, large family. It felt good to be home.

As she stacked the dishes near the dishwasher, Rennie ran from the room, Mom on her heels. When Solana looked over to where Rennie had been standing, she caught Raina's grim expression.

"I don't mean to hurt her." Then she ran from the room too.

Solana grabbed Aunt Catalina's hand. "Let's pray for them. Right now."

"Si."

River, Brisa, Madison, and Heidi joined them. Solana started the prayer, asking for the Lord to heal any rift between Rennie and Raina. Others added to the prayer. Patience for Raina. Understanding on both sides. Health of the baby and Rennie. Solana wasn't sure how long they prayed, but when they finished, she knew God would be with both of the women through the surrogacy and the months ahead.

She also sensed God reminding her He was with her too. She must trust Him to guide Adan and to give her patience.

18

"BREAKFAST, BUD!" ADAN hollered up to his son. A muffled "coming", filtered down to him.

When Jet appeared in the kitchen, Adan poured a bowl of his favorite cereal and drenched it in milk before setting it in front of him. He swallowed a bite of the cardboard flavored breakfast sandwich he had nuked a minute ago. He sure missed the hearty, flavorful meals at the dining hall on the ranch. Or the ones Lanni cooked in Albuquerque.

"You boxed up the last of your things?"

"Yeah, Dad."

Adan pounded a fist against his chest as he choked on his tolerable breakfast. Jet calling him "Dad" surprised him. Hadn't done that before. A rush of fatherly love filled him and he side hugged his son.

"Thanks, bud."

Jet squirmed, and Adan released him. His son scarfed down the cereal in record time, while Adan filled his travel mug with the dregs of coffee from the pot. Glancing at his watch, he swallowed the last bite of the breakfast sandwich.

"Put your bowl in the sink. We gotta hurry."

The *duh* look on his son's face caused his chest to expand, reminding him of the day they met—the day that changed his life for the better. Now, a month later, he couldn't imagine his life without his son.

Adan jogged up the stairs and grabbed the box. "Jet!

Suitcase!"

Jet passed him on the stairs, quickly following behind with his school backpack and the suitcase.

"Bye, Mama!" Adan called out.

She hurried out from the den. "Oh, no you don't! You can't sneak off without giving me my hugs and kisses. That goes for you too, Jet."

They both complied. Then Mama held the door open as Jet darted down the porch stairs.

"Thanks for everything, Mama. We'll see you Sunday at church."

Mama placed a hand on Adan's cheek. "You're a good father. I'm so proud of you."

Adan's throat clogged. He cleared the emotion from it before he mumbled something about needing to hurry if he was gonna meet the movers after dropping Jet at school.

"Love you both!"

Mama waved from the shade of the porch as Adan dropped the box in the bed of his truck. He locked the tonneau cover before climbing behind the wheel and pulling away from his childhood home. A mixture of joy and sadness filled his heart. Today, he and his son began a new chapter, moving into their house overlooking the valley next to the Vargas Guest Ranch and Resort.

A pinch in his gut reminded him of who wasn't moving with them: Lanni. Every time he thought about her, a warmth radiated from his chest, spreading throughout his entire body. It felt as if his heart was expanding, pulsating with a renewed sense of life. The mere thought of her brought a smile to his face, causing his cheeks to warm.

But along with the joy came a gentle ache that tugged at his core. It was as if an invisible thread connected them, a constant reminder of their separation. His longing manifested itself physically, causing his muscles to tense and his heart to ache.

He wanted to ask her to be his wife. Bought the ring

with Jet days ago after work. Thought about the timing and came up short every time. Warring thoughts between his heart's desire and putting his son first threatened to rip him apart. Part of him saw the wisdom of settling into a routine with Jet in their new home. The other part of him simply felt that life separated from Lanni made no sense at all. She belonged in his house, at his side.

"Dad, you missed the turn."

Crud. Of all the days Jet could choose to call him "dad." As if his soul wasn't already twisted in an emotional storm.

"Sorry."

He slowed and swung wide, u-turning in the middle of the street. Within a few minutes, he stopped at the curb in front of the school. Jet jumped down from the passenger side and darted inside.

Before Adan shifted into gear, a woman waved at him and approached his truck. He glanced at the clock on his phone, feeling the pressure of running late. Then he rolled down the passenger window.

"You're Jet's dad, right?"

"Yeah."

"I'm Tyler's mom, Kenzie."

"Name's Adan."

"I just wanted to thank you for asking Jet to email the apology to Tyler about their fight a few weeks ago. The whole thing was really Tyler's fault." She glanced away. "He's a handful. Anyway, I've met no one who would do what you and Jet did. I really appreciate it. And it's made it easier to talk to Tyler about his role in it. I think he's trying to change. Not saying our sons will ever be besties, but what you did... Thanks."

Adan replied, "Just trying to live out the example Jesus set for us. If you ever need anything, you've got my info."

Kenzie's face lit up. "That's so nice of you to say. Thank you."

"Not just saying it. I mean it." Then he winked at her.

"Us parents of tweeners need to stick together."

She laughed. "Ain't that the truth? Thanks again."

When she stepped back from his vehicle, he drove away.

Almost immediately, Lanni filled his thoughts again. He hadn't talked to her for a few days, so he asked his smart phone to text her that today was moving day.

Her reply pinged. He pressed the button for his hands-free system to read it to him. *Sorry can't be there. Rennie out sick.*

Adan tapped the phone icon. Lanni picked it up on the first ring.

"Miss you," he said, voice laden heavy with his love.

"Aw. Miss you too."

"What's wrong with Rennie?"

"Morning sickness. Raina is freaking out."

"Must be hard for her to sit on the sidelines while Rennie carries her child."

"Yeah. It is." Her voiced muffled. "Sorry, gotta go. Love you. Maybe I can stop by after work?"

"I'd like that. Love you."

The line went dead.

Buying a house close to the ranch had been a great idea—not just because Lanni loved it, but also because it was less than a ten-minute drive. Knowing she lived close by made him happy, though no way near as happy as if she married him.

A nudge from the Spirit reminded Adan to pray, so he did. He asked God to show him the right timing and to help him be patient in the waiting.

When he pulled into the driveway, the moving truck sat waiting. He cut the engine and quickly unlocked the house.

"Sorry. Hope you weren't waiting long."

The driver smiled. "Not to worry. We just arrived."

Adan walked them through the house, naming off the rooms. As the movers placed Annabel's furniture around the space, he realized he would need to purchase a lot more furniture. The couch and easy chairs would make more sense in the room Lanni had called the playroom. Oh well. He'd go shopping with her later to figure it all out. 'Cause no way would he pick it out on his own.

As soon as the movers left, he unpacked the truck. Then he grabbed a bottled water from the fridge, glad Lanni suggested he stock it yesterday evening. She really was the smart one.

He shook off thoughts of her as he climbed into his truck and drove to work. He'd unpack in the evening, feeling a little guilty about how much time he'd already missed from work. Dylan had been very accommodating, adjusting Adan's schedule so he could shuttle Jet to and from school.

After locking up the house, Adan glanced at the clock, a knot forming in his stomach. He was gonna be late again. Hopefully Dylan would understand.

Parking near the stables, Adan noticed Dylan speaking with some guests. He jumped out of his truck, his long legs devouring the distance. Dylan gave a slight shake of his head, indicating he didn't need help to talk to the group of women. Adan listened as his friend's stutter remained under control. He knew how hard Dylan worked with his speech pathologist and with his wife to maintain control. A sense of pride ballooned in his chest. His sister was a true helpmate for Dylan.

Just like Lanni was to him.

The thought sobered Adan as the familiar longing washed over him. He had it bad.

Parker Quaid brought out two horses, so Adan hurried inside, retrieving two more horses. He thanked Parker as they passed in the alley.

"Trixie Wind is ready too."

"Much obliged."

Adan retrieved his treasured mare and joined the guests outside. After relaying some safety instructions, he and Parker helped them mount. Then he swung into Trixie Wind's saddle and started the trail ride. It felt good to be back at work, knowing he and Jet had their own home now.

His work responsibilities included horse care, leading trail rides, assisting with equine therapy, and conducting Bible studies for recovering athletes at the sports center. He and Dylan also ran a charity related to the equine therapy they provided for disabled kids. They needed to finish the planning for their Christmas Gala fundraiser soon.

He loved being part of the impressive operation the Vargases had built. Now, if life would only settle down so he could determine when to propose to Lanni.

SOLANA HELD BACK a groan. For the third day in a row, Rennie woke with terrible morning sickness. It worried Solana so much she called her mom, asking her to stop by to determine if Rennie should go to the doctor or not. Mom said nothing sounded out of the norm, but thankfully drove her sister into town for an appointment, anyway.

While her mom's help eased some of Solana's worry, it did nothing to help with the pressure she felt trying to fill Rennie's shoes by managing the resort. Thank goodness she still had five months to shadow her big sister before the baby arrived and Rennie's leave began.

Static broke through the silence on the two-way radio the maids used. "Overflowing toilet in room 306."

Ugh.

"On it," she replied, before she remembered their handyman was off for the day. She called her cousin Dalton, the ranch manager.

"Dalton, Rennie is off sick. Who is our back up for Raul?"

"Can you call Sawyer Fullerton? Rennie said she was going to make sure he could fill in."

"Thanks."

She found his contact info on her phone and tapped on it. Long before Solana worked at the resort office, Sawyer had been their handyman. After he met his wife, he started his own renovation company with her. A perfect match for her interior design business.

"Solana, hey, how's it going?"

"I'm hoping Rennie talked to you about being on call today?"

"Uh. No, she didn't."

Solana's stomach tightened. "Please tell me you aren't onsite in the Phoenix area today."

"Nope. Just watching the kids while Cara is meeting with a client. What's going on?"

"We have an overflowing toilet in one room."

"If you can turn off the water valve for it, I can be there in about an hour."

"Yes, thank you."

She hung up and darted outside to the golf cart. Whizzing through the property, she jerked it to a stop near the room. Taking the stairs two at a time, she dug the master keycard from her back pocket. She swung the door open, relieved to see housekeeping had already turned off the valve, and left a pile of towels to soak up the water. Guess she should have asked. Would have saved her the panic.

The day turned into a series of fires needing Solana's attention. The overflowing toilet in 306 ended up needing all new parts in the tank. Thankfully, Sawyer repaired it quickly. Then one housekeeper called off sick for the afternoon. An angry customer threatened to leave if she didn't find them a room without a "herd of elephants overhead," and an accident on the highway rerouted traffic through Forepaugh. Several travelers took a wrong turn and ended up at the resort, wondering how to find their way back. Eventually, Solana called Dalton to see if Uncle Tres could sit at the property entrance, directing traffic away from the resort. On the plus side, a few families toured the resort and stayed for a meal in the dining hall or grabbed coffee and a danish at Candi's bakery.

By the time Solana made a new sign with her phone number for after hours guest services, she could hardly wait to put her feet up at home. She locked the office door and headed over to the dining hall.

Thoughts of Adan and Jet had her boxing up three meals instead. She drove up the private drive to her dream home — er, Adan's house. A few seconds after ringing the doorbell, Jet threw the door open. She held the food over her head just in time for it to miss being squished by his exuberant hug. She swore he'd grown another two inches in the last week.

"Dad! Lanni's here and she brought food!"

Adan appeared from the owner's suite, tugging a t-shirt down to his waist. His damp hair stood at all angles, clearly having showered at the end of his workday. He padded straight for her. Looping an arm around her waist, he drew her close and planted a tender kiss on her lips. Mmm. The smell of his spicy body wash sent her pulse humming.

Then he took the food from her, setting it on the kitchen counter.

"Thanks for bringing this. We're starving, and I wasn't sure if we were gonna have hot dogs or chicken nuggets." He opened a container and inhaled deeply. "Yeah, Chef's cooking trumps anything I could make."

Solana giggled as she shed the stress of the long day like a coat, mentally tucking it away in a closet. Just seeing her guys renewed her energy.

"Jet, can you get us some plates and silverware?" Adan asked. "Let's eat at the table like…"

Her heart raced as her gaze snagged on his. *Like a family.* She knew exactly what was on his mind.

"You want water, iced tea, or soda?"

"I'll take whatever soda you have. I've earned it today."

Adan scoffed. "I heard we had a bunch of lost tourists

on property."

"Yeah. That and half a dozen other crises. Rennie does way more than I ever knew. And how she stays upbeat and friendly in the face of it all, I do not know."

Adan placed their drinks on the counter and drew her into his arms. "The Lanni I know is calm and collected under pressure, too."

"Maybe. I certainly didn't feel it inside."

Jet carried two plates heaped full of food to the table. Adan held a chair for Solana and insisted she sit while he fixed her a plate. Then he placed it in front of her before taking a seat at the head of the table. He held her hand and Jet's while he prayed for them, bringing back fond memories of similar meals in Albuquerque.

Her breath caught in her throat as the desire to become a genuine family engulfed her. She watched Jet shovel food into his mouth as if someone might steal his plate.

"Taste it, bud."

"Am starving."

Adan raised an eyebrow as he stared at his son. Jet chewed slower, the interaction wrapping around her heart like a soft blanket. When Adan turned his attention to her, Solana shook off her yearning and ate a bite.

"How long can you stay?"

She puffed her cheeks before expelling the air. "Honestly, after the crazy day I've had, I hadn't planned on coming by." She offered a sweet smile. "Now that I'm here, I'm not eager to leave."

Adan curled his fingers around her hand. "We have a lot of unpacking to do tonight, so I'll understand if you want to bail."

"I can help."

"Let's finish dinner first. I won't hold you to it."

Once they were done, Jet loaded the dishes into the dishwasher. Then he shifted from foot to foot. "Dad, can I call Zack? I want to show him my new room."

Adan glanced at his phone. "Soon. Let's get this kitchen stuff unpacked first."

"So not fair," Jet grumbled.

Solana hid her smile behind her hand.

"What are you laughing at?" Adan asked as he looked up from the boxes on the counter.

She tried to school her face. "Nothing."

"Jet, go finish unpacking your room. I'll text Chrissy to see if they are done with supper."

Solana opened and closed several cabinets, getting familiar with the kitchen layout while the faint beeps confirmed Adan texted someone on his phone.

"So it looks like you unpacked at least one box."

"Jet did. I'm not sure if I'll keep stuff where he put it. I think he thought if he put stuff away before I got out of the shower, it would mean supper would be ready sooner. He does not know what a terrible cook I am."

She giggled. "So, what you're saying is you are extremely glad I brought food from the dining hall."

When he erased the distance between them, she sucked in a sharp breath.

"You have no idea," he whispered in her ear, sending currents down her spine.

Then he dropped a chaste kiss on her lips before releasing her. She missed the comfort of his arms instantly.

Adan opened the boxes of kitchen items and eyed them warily.

Solana hip bumped him out of the way. "I can do this. Why don't you let Jet call Zack?"

"Are you sure?"

"Positive."

"Thanks."

Solana pulled her hair back into a ponytail, glad she typically kept a band in her pocket. Then she emptied the box, setting everything on the counter. She surveyed the cabinets before she stowed items in what she considered the proper place, including the plates and glasses Jet had haphazardly put away earlier. Unfortunately, Annabel's utensil drawer organizers left huge empty spaces in the wide drawers. Solana decided she would order some new ones online as a housewarming gift.

Hoping to borrow a measuring tape, she peered into the owner's suite and didn't see Adan, so she walked down to the other rooms. Adan's voice filtered toward her in soft tones.

"Let's put this picture on your dresser for now. We can hang pictures tomorrow and we'll plan something nice for all these ribbons, trophies, and buckles. 'Kay?"

When she neared the entrance to Jet's room, she watched him nod before hugging Adan. Oh, how she wished it was her right to make it into a family hug. Jet released his dad and stepped back. He must have seen her, because he darted in her direction.

"Lanni, come see this picture of my mama." He grabbed her hand and dragged her towards his dresser.

She studied the picture for several seconds. "This is a lovely picture of her." Annabel smiled at the photographer from atop Silver Streak, love clearly visible in her eyes.

"Did you take this picture?"

"Yeah. Zack's mama helped me print and frame it. It was our... Last ride together before Mama got sick."

"Did you want to tell me about it?"

Jet shrugged and pursed his lips, eyes glistening. Solana crooked an arm around his shoulders for a side hug, pressing her lips to the top of his head.

"Maybe some other time?"

Jet nodded. The solemnness hung in the air, so Solana gave him one more squeeze before releasing him. As she looked up, she saw the yearning in Adan's eyes before he masked it. She jerked her head toward the hall and he followed her out to the great room.

"You are amazing with him." Adan's husky voice communicated so much more than his words. He admired her—maybe even saw her as motherly.

Solana allowed the compliment to bounce off her heart, too afraid to let it root there while their relationship remained unclear.

"I wanted to see if you have a tape measure so I can find better organizers for the kitchen drawers."

"Lanni." His hand slid down her arm and he nudged her to face him. Then he reached up and rested his palm against her cheek. "You being here… It's right and good and… It's getting harder and harder to spend life apart from you. Jet needs you."

His last words pierced her heart. As much as she wanted to be there for Jet, it was Adan's heart she had hoped to win. Her eyes dropped to the floor.

"Look at me."

When she did, her breath caught at the storm of desire and tender love written in his gorgeous blue eyes.

"I love you so much. I've been praying about us and I think God never intended for me to be a single dad. The picture is incomplete without you. You belong at my side."

The words sounded like what she had waited a long time to hear. Yet, something about them left her feeling uneasy and uncertain. Did Adan want her as his wife or as a mother to his son?

"I…"

Adan pressed his finger on her lips. "Let me take you to dinner tomorrow night?"

She nodded as her pulse quickened.

"Just you and me."

"Alright."

"Now, you've already helped a ton tonight. Why don't you head on home and relax?"

He leaned forward and brushed his lips across hers. Not once, but twice, before he escorted her to the door.

"See you tomorrow."

"Night, Adan."

Then she drove back to her apartment on the ranch, emotions still churning. Feeling like a buoy without an anchor, bobbing up and down on the harsh waves, desperate for clarity.

19

THE NEXT MORNING, Solana frowned when Adan's name popped on her phone screen while she was training Teri how to add another day to a guest's existing reservation. It was a complicated process, so she quickly swiped her phone to ignore the call. When he immediately called back, she apologized to Teri and the guest before answering.

"Adan, can I call you back?"

"Lanni?" Jet's voice unexpectedly sounded on the other end, laced with fear. "Something is wrong with Dad."

She mouthed the words, "Sorry. Emergency." Then she ducked into the privacy of Rennie's office.

"What's wrong, sweetie?"

"He didn't get up with his alarm and he's not waking up!"

A lump formed in her throat as she suppressed her fear. Maintaining her composure was crucial to calming him.

"What if he's dead like my mama?" Muffled sobs followed Jet's hysterical question.

"Jet. Let's take this one step at a time. Is his chest moving?"

"I can't tell."

"Okay, I'm on my way. Tell me what you see."

She pushed past the guest and a nervous Teri, grateful to catch Rennie along the path to the employee parking lot. She muted the phone and gave Rennie the five second rundown before jogging to her car.

"He moved!"

Relief flooded through her body, sending prickles along her limbs. She set her phone on the center console while she backed out and drove toward Adan's house.

"Jet, does your dad's forehead feel hot or cold?"

"It's really hot."

"He probably has a fever. Hang tight. I'm parking in the driveway now. Can you come let me in?"

"Yeah."

Then the line went dead.

Solana opened her car door as Jet flung the house door wide. His tear-streaked cheeks and pale face sent a jolt of fear through her seconds before he grabbed her arm and dragged her towards the owner's suite.

When she saw Adan, she understood why Jet had been so alarmed. His hair matted against his forehead. The ashen tone of his face contrasted starkly with the dark sheets on the bed. She crossed the room and confirmed he had a fever.

"Is he dying?"

"No, sweetie. He's probably got the flu or a terrible cold. Why don't you sit here with him and I'll be right back?"

Solana filled a glass with water in the kitchen and found some ibuprofen in the medicine cabinet. Then she settled on the edge of the bed, coaxing Adan to sit up enough to sip the water and take the medicine. He mumbled a few incoherent sounds, then obeyed before he nestled deeper into his bed.

"Come on, Jet, let's give him some space."

She finally lured the shaken boy into the great room where she called Adan's mom.

"Solana, I'm surprised to hear from you."

"Morning, Heidi. Hey, do you know how to let the school know Jet won't be in class today?"

"I do. What's wrong?"

"Adan is really sick and Jet's too distraught. I don't think he'd concentrate a lick if I drove him in."

"Oh, my. I'll let the school know. Then I'll be right over. Thanks so much for helping them both."

Heidi hung up before Solana could respond. Taking care of her guys meant everything to her. So, of course, she had come as soon as she realized Jet and Adan needed her.

She flopped down on the couch next to Jet and slung an arm over his shoulders. "He's gonna be fine. Don't worry."

Jet turned his face into her shoulder, silent sobs shaking his body, reminding her he was still a child — one who lost so much. She smoothed his hair back, whispering words of comfort while praying for him.

Some time passed when the doorbell rang. Solana stood and answered it.

"Heidi. Thanks for coming."

"Of course. I know you probably need to get back to work."

"It's no trouble."

"I know Adan will appreciate all you did to calm Jet. It can't be easy seeing his dad laid low after everything with his mom."

Heidi hugged Jet and sent him out to her car to bring in some grocery sacks.

"I'll make my chicken soup for Adan. I also brought this." Heidi held up a test kit for the flu, RSV, etc. "Do you know if he has telehealth?"

"Yeah. I'll make sure the app is installed on his phone."

Solana creeped into the bedroom to get it. Adan stirred.

"Lanni?"

"Trying to get out of our date, huh?"

Adan groaned. "I'm sorry. Raincheck?"

"Sure. Your mom is here, and we kept Jet home from school. He's a wreck."

"Send him in for a minute?"

Solana poked her head out of the room and motioned for Jet. While he sat on the edge of the bed, she leaned against the doorway.

"I'm just sick, bud. Nothing to worry about. One lady on the trail ride had a bit of a cold yesterday, and I probably caught whatever she was recovering from. Was up most of the night coughing and am worn out."

Jet threw his arms around Adan's neck, hugging him tight.

Solana slipped from the room, heart heavy over the situation. Heidi promised to keep her informed of Adan's progress before she left.

As she drove back to work, she prayed for Adan and Jet. Her deepest desire was to stay to care for them both. If Adan didn't propose to her soon, she might have to take matters into her own hands.

ON MONDAY MORNING, Adan woke to a quiet house. A sticky note on his side table informed him his mama took Jet to school. Adan eased out of bed and headed for the shower. His head pounded and a coughing fit nearly brought him to his knees. When it passed, he opted for some medicine before showering. By the time he finished dressing for his day, he plopped onto the couch and closed his eyes.

Some time later, he stirred to the aroma of coffee and bacon. His stomach grumbled, propelling him to his feet. His mama's back faced him as she flitted around the kitchen.

"Morning."

She glanced over her shoulder. "You feel up for some breakfast?"

"Yup. Thanks for taking care of me."

"I'm glad to see you on the mend. Haven't seen you sick like that since you were a little boy. It's going on four days."

"I feel like I…" Coughs shook his body. He sounded like a barking dog.

"Solana was here."

He knew that tone — the one that said Mama knew something she wasn't saying.

"When?"

"Friday. Jet called her when you missed your alarm."

"I vaguely remember." Adan scrubbed his hands on his face. "Must have scared him."

"It did, but we talked through it."

Mama pushed a plate of food toward him. He settled on the bar stool on the other side of the counter. Her face brightened as she absentmindedly wiped down the countertop.

"He calls me Nana now. I love it."

Adan snorted. "Not Granny?"

His mother's rounded eyes and arched eyebrows sent a warning. "Heavens no. I'm not old enough to be a granny."

He scrunched his nose, letting the topic go.

"So…" Mama hedged. "When are you gonna admit you love Solana and marry her and give your son a new mama?"

The barrage of questions pelted his heart. "I love her. Have the ring. Waiting —" Another round of coughs interrupted him. He drank some water before continuing. "Right time." He shrugged.

"Humph. You two have been friends for years and have been in love as long. Just marry her already."

"Mama!?"

She grinned sheepishly, almost a mirror image of his similar expression.

"I'm not normally one in favor of a brief engagement. You two? It's like you've been dating for five years without admitting it. Don't waste more time."

Adan considered her words as he finished the meal.

"Another thing… Don't miss a 'good' time to propose while searching for the elusive 'perfect' time."

"Good advice. Thanks Mama."

He stood, exhaustion tugging at him. So she sent him back to bed. He fell asleep to sweet thoughts of his Lanni.

20

———————

THREE MORE DAYS passed before Adan felt human again. His mother's advice nagged at his conscience. He was long past the point of guessing if he should propose. His prayers had been confirmed in a conversation with his dad yesterday. Dad's one piece of advice was to ask for Diego Vargas's permission before asking Solana. It might be old-fashioned, but Adan would gladly honor Diego. He ended up texting Diego to see if they could meet for a late lunch at *The Lariat*, a western bistro in town.

When he opened the door to the restaurant, he quickly spotted Diego sitting in a booth, sipping a coffee. Adan crossed the room and greeted him with a hug, having known him his entire life. His dad was a close friend of both Tres and Diego Vargas. The Francos spent many Sunday afternoons and holidays with the Vargases.

"Adan, how are you feeling? Lanni said you were pretty sick."

"Much better. A bit of a lingering cough, but nothing contagious."

"I hope you don't mind, I ordered. Don't want to leave Katie short-staffed at the feed store for too long."

"No worries."

Aunt Greta, the owner, swung by to fill a mug with coffee for Adan and took his order. "It'll be ready in a few minutes."

When she left, Adan squirmed in the booth, suddenly nervous. He cleared his throat and said a brief prayer silently.

"Thanks for meeting me on short notice."

"Is this about Lanni?"

"Yes. I wanted to ask for your blessing. She… I love her with all my heart and I believe she feels as strongly about me. I hope to ask her to be my wife, but couldn't picture it without first coming to you."

Diego took a slow drink of his coffee, studying Adan with narrowed eyes. Adan held his gaze despite the tension wrapping around his stomach. Then Diego rubbed a hand down his face, sighing loudly.

"I thought I was ready for this. Half expected someone to ask for Rennie or Lanni's hand. Son, daughters will give you no end of stress."

Adan's heart threatened to stop beating as Diego worked through his own thoughts aloud.

"I had a feeling something like this might happen when she insisted on going to Albuquerque with you."

"Nothing happened."

Diego scoffed. "I don't think that's true. I think you finally woke up to the fact that you've loved my little girl —" Diego sucked in a sharp breath and his throat worked. "That you've loved Lanni for years."

Adan's heart pounded in his ears and perspiration dotted his forehead, nervous that Diego didn't see him as a fit match.

"I know I'm a decade older than her. I was hung up on that for a while. Didn't think she'd want me. Now? I can't imagine life without her. She loves me. She loves my son."

Diego held up his hand, a stern expression stopping Adan. "I know you love each other. I had a feeling when she went with you that God would use the trip to make you see He destined you for a long life together."

Adan straightened in his seat, trying to make sense of

the words.

"What I'm trying to say, Adan, is that Katie and I are happy to give you our blessing. Solana is the perfect help-mate for you, and you are for her. She'll be a wonderful mother to Jet and any other children that come along."

Adan blinked. Then a grin pushed across his face as his heart threatened to soar right out of his body. "Thank you, Diego."

Diego glanced behind Adan and nodded. Aunt Greta deposited their sandwiches on the table and quickly refilled their coffee. When she rested a hand on Adan's shoulder, she smiled down at him.

"About time you and Solana made it official. Congratulations."

Adan snorted. "Still have to ask her."

Aunt Greta chuckled as she walked away.

Diego held his gaze. "Make it soon. Oh, Katie said we'd be fine with a quick engagement, given how long you've been friends and with your son and all."

Adan thanked him, even though Diego's words didn't quite match his expression. His earlier comment about daughters started to make sense. Adan could see his future father-in-law's deep love for Lanni.

Now, all Adan had to do was find a good time to propose.

SOLANA WIPED HER forehead on her sleeve, the afternoon sun warming her as she balanced on a stepladder to fix some of the harvest festival decorations. The unseasonably warm late-November weather caused her to wish for a short-sleeve t-shirt instead of the long-sleeve snap front. At least her cowgirl hat shaded her face and neck.

"A little to the right," Rennie instructed from behind

her. "Good."

Solana held back a frustrated growl. Normally, Rennie would help. But Devon and Raina would have freaked out to see her on any ladder, even a two-foot one. She shook her head as she climbed down.

Too bad Adan was out on a trail ride. His height would be an advantage for her current task. An early winter storm blew through last night, leaving many of the decorations in disarray. The seasonal wranglers spent an hour scraping up hay that had broken loose off the bales. Even Catalina Vargas and her daughter-in-law River came to help straighten upended displays.

After another hour, Solana surveyed the harvest festival grounds. It looked good enough for the last weekend before Thanksgiving. Next weekend, all the fall decor would go back to storage and Christmas would appear almost overnight. At least, that's how the guests perceived the transition. To the staff, the project required tons of overtime, volunteers galore, and infinite patience.

With two of her cousin's wives and Rennie in their second trimesters, Solana felt the pressure to step up even more. Since Thanksgiving fell so late this year, the turnaround must happen before the Christmas Gala for Adan and Dylan's charity, Braden's Hope. They had scheduled it for two days after Thanksgiving.

Her eyes stung, feeling utterly overwhelmed. She missed Adan and Jet desperately. She hated that time with them had been limited to quick video calls or a hurried lunch between tasks. By the time she crawled into bed daily, she fell asleep fast, weary to the bone.

Solana scuffed along the pea gravel path to *Candi's Coffee & Sweets*, needing a caffeine boost to make it through the rest of the afternoon. Head down, she shrieked when an arm wrapped around her waist. Swirling in the air, it took her a second to recognize Adan. The overpowering scent of horse hung around him. Only the tiniest hint of his musky body wash remained.

"Mmm. You smell amazing," he said as he set her feet on the ground, nuzzling her neck with his nose.

"Amazingly bad? I feel sticky and gross."

Adan leaned back. "Nope. You're perfect."

She rolled her eyes, too exhausted to joke around.

He waggled his eyebrows. "Kiss me."

Solana's shoulders rose and fell with a resigned breath.

"Uh, oh. What's wrong, Lanni?"

She twisted out of his embrace, clasping his hand as she continued to the coffee shop. "I need a pick me up and not the kind you have in mind."

His chuckle warmed her heart. "I'm happy to buy you a coffee."

"And a cake pop?"

"Or two. I promise not to tell anyone."

After she ordered, Adan pointed her toward a table in front of the massive window. "Sit. I'll bring it to you."

Solana grabbed a few napkins and dampened them with water before taking a seat. She dabbed the cool napkins on her face and neck, feeling somewhat refreshed. Adan placed their coffees and a handful of cake pops on the table. Then he turned his chair backwards and rested his arms on the seatback. He unwrapped a chocolate cake pop and held it in front of her mouth.

"Eat."

She screwed up her face. When he pressed it against her lips, she opened her mouth and bit off the entire pop from the holder. She finished chewing, and Adan slid the pumpkin latte toward her. He winked as she sipped it. After he unwrapped two more cake pops, he handed her a vanilla one. Then he clinked his against hers in a mock toast before stuffing it in his mouth. Somehow, he managed a megawatt grin while chewing.

Solana ate the second one, savoring it. The sweet sugar perked her up.

"Now, tell me what's on your mind."

After another sip of her latte, she finally spoke. "I miss you. I miss Jet."

Adan's smile lit his entire face. "We miss you too."

A weird expression flitted across his face before he stood. Then, without warning, he dropped to one knee, clutching her hand.

"Solana Vargas—"

A loud squeal came from the counter before Candi moved closer, phone held high.

"I have loved you for more years than I can count. You are my heart. I think of you all the time and can barely stand each day that passes without you by my side."

Solana's heart slammed against her chest as she sucked in a sharp breath. He was doing this now? She must look a sight.

Adan dug into his pocket and produced a shiny gold ring with three diamonds. He slid it onto the tip of her ring finger.

"Lanni, will you be my wife? Will you complete my family? Will you walk with me through the chaos and through the quiet times?"

Tears sprang to her eyes, dribbling down her cheeks. Her other hand rested over her heart. She nodded emphatically, words stuck in her throat.

"This center diamond represents you, the center of our family. The one on the right is me, and the one on the left is Jet. He wanted you to know he wants you to be his step-mom and that any ring had to remind you he chooses you too. And the gold band represents God holding us together."

A sob. Then she blubbered as she launched into Adan's waiting arms. She pressed her lips against his for a kiss that communicated a more emphatic "yes" than words ever could.

When her emotions settled, she released her hold on the love of her life. Then she play-punched his biceps.

"You smell like horse."

Adan tossed his head back and laughed deeply. "Those are the words you manage to say? Not 'yes'?"

"It's not exactly the ideal time or place for a proposal."

He shrugged before pulling her against his chest. "Mama said not to miss a 'good' time waiting for the 'perfect', so I took her advice."

Solana shook her head and narrowed her eyes. "You."

Then he captured her lips in a kiss that set the world spinning and her heart soaring. She finally had Adan Franco's ring on her finger. Now for the babies of their own part. Or a wedding first, then that.

Epilogue

One Week Later

RENATA VARGAS STARED into the full-length mirror in her bedroom, rubbing her hand over the clearly visible baby bump. Those mixed emotions bubbled to the surface, causing her to wonder for the hundredth time why she had volunteered to be a surrogate for her cousin Devon and his wife Raina. Sympathy over Raina's inability to conceive naturally—her endometriosis having scarred her years before meeting Devon.

No, it had been more than sympathy. She had prayed over the decision for nearly four months before talking to her doctor to learn more. Then another month before going to Devon and Raina to see if they wanted to pursue surrogacy.

She sighed as she slid the green patterned maternity dress over her changing body. The initial flutters started yesterday and freaked her out. Mom assured her the banana-sized child in her belly would feel like that.

A growing pang squeezed Renata's heart tight. The longer she carried the child, the more attached she felt to him, even though he wasn't hers. He was one hundred percent the product of Devon and Raina's DNA. She provided the place for him to grow and be born into the world—some time around April—still four months away.

A knock sounded at the door. "Rennie? Are you ready?"

She blinked back the burning of her eyes at Solana's question. Was she ready to birth the baby that wasn't hers? Was she ready to not stand next to her sister on Solana's wedding day? Was she ready for fluctuating hormones? No. She wasn't ready for any of it. Not emotionally.

Renata scraped her black hair back and secured it in a high ponytail before opening the door. She hugged her sister to mask her efforts to paste on a smile she didn't feel.

"Let's get you to your groom."

Solana's smile stretched wide across her lips.

A pinch of both joy and jealousy rose. Renata shouldn't envy Solana's happy day. Watching her younger sister pine over Adan for years, she was truly happy for her finally winning Adan's heart.

Solana let out a shaky breath as they piled into Renata's white Jeep Wrangler. If the little baby were going to be hers, she might consider getting rid of the Wrangler in favor of one with a wider back door—something easier to manage a baby seat.

"I'm gonna be a wife and mother by the end of the day."

Renata reached over and squeezed her sister's hand. She forced a light tone. "I'm so happy for you. You and Adan are great together. Jet is lucky to have you as his new mom."

"What if I mess up?"

Renata snorted. "You remember our parents, right? I'm sure you will. Trust God and trust your husband. You'll figure it out."

Solana scoffed. "Always the pragmatist."

Renata shrugged before backing out. Then she drove them to the church. If Lanni only knew how incredibly conflicted she felt inside. Doubting every choice. Hating herself for wishing Devon and Raina's baby were really hers. Four more months of this self-doubt and second guessing.

The next few hours blurred. Renata kicked off her sandals, hoping her feet wouldn't swell too much more. She watched as Adan stood at the front of the church in one of his fine suits and a dark cowboy hat. The love on his face made it radiant.

Then everyone stood, Renata stuffing her fat feet back into her sandals, as Dad walked Solana down the aisle toward the man she had loved for five years. Perhaps longer. Their secret love and long friendship made the wedding seem less rushed than it could have with only a one-week engagement.

Solana handed her bouquet to a friend from high school. That should have been Renata's place had she not been five months pregnant. What else would she miss? How much more would she sacrifice to bring Devon and Raina joy for a lifetime?

Tears dampened Adan's cheeks as he looked down into Solana's eyes, pledging his whole life and self to her. She gazed upon him with deep adoration.

Renata dug around for a tissue in her purse and dabbed the corner of her eyes. Maybe the pregnancy caused her to be more emotional than normal. Or maybe it was her heart still hurting over the rejection and betrayal from a lying cowboy. Some year she ought to let it go. Especially if she wanted to have a family of her own.

When the pastor presented Adan and Solana to the crowd, Adan slipped one hand at Solana's waist and the other cupped her cheek. Then he kissed her tenderly before releasing her. He clasped her hand and grinned like a smitten fool.

Would any man ever feel like that about her? Renata forced a smile as her sister and brother-in-law walked past her, shoving the thought aside. It would be several months after the birth before her body would return to normal. No way would she date while pregnant with someone else's child.

Besides, the right man for her would be too honorable to fall for her in this state. It would be messy and complicated.

How would she explain surrogacy and why she volunteered for it?

Jet wrapped Solana in a long embrace at the back of the church, causing moisture to dampen Renata's cheeks. Guess he was her nephew now. Or would be as soon as Solana officially adopted him. He was a good kid and deserved two loving parents after so much loss. Seemed like he was thriving now. Good.

Renata spent most of the reception seated with her feet propped on a chair next to her. The reception ended up being an outdoor event that Drake and Chef pulled together in record time. Candi baked and decorated a lovely wedding cake, too. Mom, Aunt Catalina, Heidi Franco, and all Renata's cousins' wives decorated the church and the outdoor space back at the ranch. It all turned out perfectly.

"This seat taken?" Ross Braxton asked.

Renata shook her head before he sat down across from her.

"Been meaning to ask you…" He fidgeted with an empty water glass on the table.

"Go ahead."

"My brother's ranch in Montana isn't doing so well. How would you feel about him picking your brain?"

Renata pushed aside her unfinished meal. "I think Dalton would be the better person to help. Or Derin."

"He wants to learn about what you do on the resort side. He could come down for a few months in the spring."

"I suppose he could shadow me. By then, Solana will be ready to cover for my leave, too."

"Oh, right. When's the baby due?"

She hadn't missed the flush that spread over the part of his cheeks not hidden by the beard. Devon, Raina, and she agreed she could tell the staff about her surrogacy if she wanted to. Perhaps she ought to tell Ross—especially if his brother showed up in a few months.

As the words hovered on the tip of her tongue, Solana

caught her attention.

"Let's talk more later."

Renata stood and wished her sister well before reassuring her she would take good care of Jet while Solana and Adan honeymooned at a resort in Scottsdale for a few days.

As she drove Jet to his house, she recalled Ross's request. She could probably help his brother out. Teaching him what she knew about running a resort as part of a guest ranch. Might even help distract her from her warring emotions about the baby growing inside of her.

Continue the series with Renata's story in *Falling for a Pregnant Cowgirl (Vargas Ranch Book 7).*

From the Author

Sometimes best friends who fall in love can't quite see what's right in front of them. They treasure the friendship and are afraid of what will happen if it changes. I didn't want to dwell on this point too much because it's really a multi-faceted complex set of emotions.

Adan's hang up on their age difference kept him from pursuing Solana romantically. I knew it would take a major shake up in his life to shift his perspective. The idea of giving him a son from his rodeo days seemed like a great way to accomplish this. Yet, I wanted to honor his strong faith exhibited throughout the series. I knew readers were unlikely to accept him as a thirty-five-year-old virgin, so I discarded that idea quickly. It would also be out of character for him to ignore his child's existence. In the end, I went for a somewhat unconventional way to introduce him to Jet.

The circumstances required Adan to rely on his best friend, Solana. Adan needed to see her in a different light. In the end, I felt the story could only unfold in a way where Adan was way out of his comfort zone.

Solana's childhood crush and adult friendship needed to change, too. She had to grow to rely on God and to love God more than she loved Adan. In the end, her faith grew, and her love matured into something beautiful. I also loved the way her servant's heart provided the perfect motive for her jumping to Adan's aid.

One aspect I found challenging to write about was Jet's character through Adan and Solana's eyes. I toyed with writing his point of view, but felt it could make the story feel too heavy as he worked through his grief. In the end, I'm happy with the results.

Anyway, I hope you enjoyed watching Adan and Solana finally admit their love and seeing Jet thriving after so much loss. Catch up with Renata Vargas and Gabe Braxton in *Falling for a Pregnant Cowgirl*.

Blessings,

Karen Baney

About the Author

Karen Baney is passionate about writing stories full of flawed characters. She enjoys weaving together stories of second chances, redemption, and overcoming personal trials. As a transplant to Arizona, she loves researching the state's history and finding ways to seamlessly incorporate real history and real settings into her novels. In addition to writing and speaking, Karen works as a Software Development Manager for a Christian ministry.

Her faith plays an important role both in her life and in her writing. Karen and her husband, Jim, make their home in Gilbert, Arizona, with their two dogs, Bella and Daisy. Both Jim and Karen are active at Rock Point Church in Queen Creek, Arizona.

Discover faith-laced stories with characters who feel like life-long friends.

Visit www.karenbaney.com to discover more historical romance series set in the American West. Follow Karen's writing journey and get behind-the-scenes glimpses of her research adventures on social media.

Facebook: @AuthorKarenBaney
X: @karen_baney
Instagram: @AuthorKarenBaney
BookBub: Follow Karen Baney for new release alerts

Books By Karen Baney

<u>Contemporary Romance</u>

Vargas Ranch Series:
Love is in the air at the Vargas Guest Ranch & Resort near Wickenburg, Arizona. Meet the Vargas family—five swoon-worthy brothers and their cousins who live by their family motto: "We do not deviate from the Lord's plan." These rugged cowboys run a successful working ranch and luxury resort while navigating the rollercoaster of finding true love.

Falling for a Fake Cowboy
Falling for a Real Cowboy
Honeymoon with a Real Cowboy
Falling for a Shy Cowboy
Falling for a Bossy Cowboy
Falling for a Smart Cowboy
Falling for a Humbug Cowboy
Falling for a Devoted Cowgirl
Falling for a Pregnant Cowgirl
Falling for a Cowboy's Legacy

Steadfast Love Series:
The *Steadfast Love* series follows a close-knit group of friends as they navigate the beautiful mess of modern life in the Phoenix area—workplace drama, complicated families, and love that shows up when they least expect it. These contemporary romances blend emotional depth with authentic faith, reminding us that even when life unravels, God's love never does.

The Heart I Rescue (prequel)
The Air I Breathe

Historical Western Romance

Prescott Pioneers Series:
Step back in time to the wild, untamed Arizona Territory where survival depends on grit, faith, and the courage to start over. Follow three pioneer families—the Andersons, Colters, and Larsons—as they risk everything for the promise of a new life in a land that demands both strength and hope.

A Dream Unfolding
A Heart Renewed
A Life Restored
A Hope Revealed
Hidden Prospects

Desert Manna Series:
Sometimes the most beautiful love stories bloom in the desert. Set in the growing frontier town of Prescott during the early 1870s, these tender romances follow women rebuilding their lives after heartbreak and the unexpected men who help them discover that second chances at love are worth the risk. Set in Prescott, Arizona between 1871 - 1873.

Beauty for Ashes
Joy for Mourning
Oaks of Justice

Colter Sons Series:
Power, legacy, and forbidden love collide in this sweeping family saga set in the Arizona Territory. The Colter ranch empire has weathered decades of frontier life, but now family secrets and buried betrayals threaten to destroy everything. As five brothers—and one resilient sister—navigate the treacherous waters of love, loss, and redemption, they must decide what's worth fighting for. Set in Prescott and

other locations within the Arizona Territory in 1887 - 1906.

The Reluctant Cattleman
The Roaming Adventurer
The Railroad Magnate
The Resourceful Stockman
The Restless Wrangler
The Resilient Bride

Larson Sisters Series

Meet the next generation! These delightful novellas follow the three daughters of Adam and Julia Larson from the *Prescott Pioneers Series* as they navigate love, courtship, and finding their own happily ever afters in territorial Arizona in 1886 – 1894.

In Love at Christmas
In Love with the Rancher
In Love with the Horse Trainer

Desert Life Media

Desert Life Media: *There Is Life in The Desert*

Entertainment-first Christian fiction set in the Southwest, featuring redemption, family, and faith

Publishing clean, wholesome, and uplifting fiction since 2010

---

desertlifemedia.com

www.ingramcontent.com/pod-product-compliance
Lightning Source LLC
Chambersburg PA
CBHW071907220626
47052CB00002B/251